COASTAL ACCESS

A NOVEL BY WALTER RAMSAY

Pena Beach Press

New Jersey - Florida

For information about the author and future books:
www.walterramsay.com
penabeachpress@gmail.com

Front cover illustration by Michele Ramsay

ISBN: 0-9834407-4-3
ISBN-13: 978-0-9834407-4-1
LCCN: 2012936441
Pena Beach Press, Pine Beach, NJ
Printed in the United States of America

To the next generation of Ramsays

Jack

Leah

&

Brady

CHAPTER

1

Certain days occur only once in a great while. The ones you enjoy, cherish, and secure in your memory. Mornings are glorious with clear blue skies and a sun's warmth that tickles your senses. For Andy Babcock, or Drew, as his few friends called him, this was how the beginning of his day seemed as he headed out to explore and hunt in the area that many called a wasteland; an area of Florida time forgot.

A faint mist hovered over the marshy lake region that makes up the western portion of Brevard County. The sun would gradually burn off the mist, and a magnificent spring day would arrive.

Drew saw himself as the last of his kind; a loner who loved the isolation the land provided. A purebred Floridian, Drew grew up in Cocoa, where his family had resided for as long as he could remember. The continuous growth of the area and the influx of

Northerners for the space race had gradually pushed him west of Interstate 95. It was the perfect place for someone who wanted to be left alone.

With no family to speak of, the sixty-five-year-old lived alone, hunted for his food, and gathered all the necessities he needed from the natural resources of the area. The only contact he had with the outside world came when he intermittently visited a local corner store near the main road for a few staple items and an occasional beer. He shunned every creature comfort one could have. No telephones, televisions, computers, cell phones, or World Wide Web; life was nice and simple. Everything he needed could be found in his bungalow on a dirt road off of Highway 532. People seldom, if ever, traveled the road or visited the area. For most, its only existence was on the county tax map.

Today was like every other day for Drew. He woke up early to travel deep into the underbrush, where he would check his traps, gather herbs and berries, and return home before the sun reached its zenith. Hopes were always high on catching fox, duck, or deer. The occasional gator was his only concern. However, the gators seemed to watch out for Drew as much as he watched out for them. The possibility of being skinned and turned into a stylish pocketbook seemed to be on their minds as they stayed clear of his path.

As Drew walked along that morning, an odd feeling came over him. Something felt a little different. What was it? He stood, listened, and finally heard a faint rumbling in the distance. The breeze picked up as he checked the sky for thunderheads. Ominous clouds now appeared, telling him to return home. This sudden change caught Drew by surprise, and he was seldom, if ever, surprised.

His instincts warned him to retreat, but his stubbornness persisted, so he continued to track along. The rumblings continued, and he realized there were now two sets of sounds working in unison. Drew knew the sound of thunder that was quickly approaching and finally realized the other sounds were not made by nature. On his walk the other day, he had spotted a few white trucks roaring across the remote land. It had seemed strange to him since no traffic ever came off the main roads, but he realized that these sounds were similar, something motorized.

Drew continued his stroll and focused his attention on the deer trail he was now following. He walked carefully so as not to disturb the surrounding area or leave any tracks. Yet that uneasy feeling continued to creep up on him as the rumbling noise persisted.

From the corner of his eye, Drew suddenly spotted the source of the sound as two quads rounded the bend. Within seconds, they approached and came alongside Drew.

"Hey there, buddy," one of the riders called out as they rolled to a stop. Drew quickly tightened the grip on his rifle as he looked at the two men in hunting gear with their own rifles slung over their backs. He nodded a greeting.

"We haven't seen many other hunters out here. Are you alone?" one asked with a smile.

Drew said nothing, just nodded his head again, thinking they might be poachers until he saw something that resembled a security patch on the shoulder of one of the men.

The sky continued to darken as the two men sat like statues.

"We were hoping," the smaller guy said, "that you might be able to point us in the direction of some good hunting."

Drew thought it strange for the two to be out here, especially in the approaching storm, but he answered anyway, his tone disgusted. "You're not gonna get anything with those noisy contraptions ya'll is sitting on."

"Oh, we get the whole silent hunting thing. Actually, we were hoping to set up camp, sit for a while, and wait to see what comes our way," continued the smaller of the two.

Drew thought for a moment while he watched the one who wasn't talking just stare stoically into the distance. Without further hesitation or emotion, Drew responded, "Well, ya'll could head down to Crane's Creek, about two miles south of here. It's a great place to camp. Pull out a little food, and all the pickings will come to you. But you better get a move on; that there storm is approaching faster than I ever seen."

As Drew pointed toward the south, the smaller of the two turned his head in that direction, but the other remained as still as a statue, staring straight ahead.

"You say we'll find good things down there? Guess we could give it a try," he said as he motioned to the guy next to him to get moving along. "Thank you kindly," he added.

Drew nodded in return, turned, and started down his trail, retreating home as the two strangers adjusted themselves in their seats before firing up those powerful beasts.

* * *

Birds scattered, deer stood at attention, and a single gator slid into the murky water from its embankment as two shots echoed across the vast expanse of wetlands.

The storm disappeared as quickly as it arrived, and the sounds of the two quads slowly faded into the distance as Drew Babcock lay dying with two gunshot wounds in his back.

The last thought that ran through Drew's mind as his life slowly trickled away was…*why?*

CHAPTER

2

"One more evening, honey," was the comment that slipped out of my mouth. I almost choked as I brushed my teeth while getting ready to head out for dinner. Shit, I couldn't remember the last time I called someone honey.

Karla entered the bathroom, walked up behind me, and wrapped her arms around my waist.

"I know, I'm a little sad we have to head back too," she said as she nibbled on the back of my neck. "These past ten days have been the best days I've had in a long time."

I wiped my mouth and spun around to face her. As I pressed her against me, the firmness of her breasts rested against my chest.

"You know it's been awesome for me too," I said, squeezing her even tighter before placing a soft kiss on her forehead.

"I still can't believe how amazing you always look," I whispered as I gently pushed her an arm's distance away and spun her around like she was a tiny dancer in a jewelry box.

Karla wore an emerald print round-neck dress with button fastenings and a tie in the back; a long slit in the front accentuated her long, tanned legs. Her green eyes sparkled, their softness matching the shade of her dress, while her long, dark hair framed her oval face. I again pulled her tightly to me, feeling every curve of her body against mine.

"You look like a photo from a catalog," I murmured and knew my choice of words to flatter her may have come across as a little clumsy.

"Thank you." She smiled and took my hand as we headed out the door toward Duval Street to hit downtown Key West.

The walk through town and down to the square was short and enjoyable. We stopped to check out the street kiosks and occasional souvenir tourist trap.

Our destination, Mallory Square, had its usual collection of characters, sideshows, and people from all over the globe. We bought overpriced cocktails in plastic cups from a street vendor and sipped them as we walked, taking in the sights, waiting for the legendary Key West sunset.

"A beautiful evening, as usual," Karla said with a giggle as a silver statue came to life and motioned to us as we walked by.

"It sure is, but the damn price for this watered-down excuse for alcohol is ridiculous." I had done quite well financially from my newspaper exposés, but I was not in any frame of mind to throw it away either.

Karla laughed, and we found a spot to watch the sunset. It was a spectacular sight, the reddish glow accentuating the scattered clouds lying low on the horizon. As the sun lowered, the crowd became completely silent, as if hoping to hear the sun sizzle as it slowly disappeared into the gulf.

After a quiet dinner at Schooner's Wharf and a stroll along the dock, we made a quick stop at Jimmy Buffett's Margaritaville for a nightcap. Our walk back to the room was even more enjoyable, with short stops for a little nibble off each other. The night was perfect. A gentle breeze, clear skies, and stars that looked close enough to reach out and touch. The palms gently swayed, sounding as if they were whispering love songs. The evening scene had evolved absolutely perfectly, complete with a beautiful woman by my side.

Okay, one thing was better: entering the bedroom with Karla. We were both feeling no pain as we barely closed the door behind us. Karla slowly let her dress drop, and her fingers ran along my manhood as she pushed me onto the bed and slowly removed my shorts. We had been here ten days, and every night had been more amazing than the one prior.

As my face nuzzled against her soft skin, I slowly cupped her breast and rotated my tongue around her erect nipple, making her body arch under me. Her slow, rhythmic thrusts made me struggle to hold back the explosion raging to be released inside me. Once she straddled me, we continued rocking back and forth until we climaxed together. As total exhaustion overcame us, we fell into a deep, restful sleep.

CHAPTER

3

The haze slowly cleared in Tucker's dream as he found himself alone on a dune. It was not the one of his previous dreams from a few months ago, that was for certain. Rather, it was one that overlooked a golden beach and the turquoise-blue water of the Atlantic.

He stood without the usual feeling of anxiety; this was different. There was no thunder, lightning, or darkness. It was a beautiful day, the type the Space Coast usually had to offer. Tucker felt relieved. A feeling of contentment washed over him. He slowly floated along the ridge and above the sea grass, enjoying his present state of mind.

A refreshing breeze blew in from the west as the sun on his face warmed his entire being. He could not understand why there were no people on the stretch of beach enjoying such a lovely day.

Relishing the moment, Tucker suddenly noticed a figure—no, three figures—strolling along the shoreline. They were walking casually, kicking up the sand and playing tag with the fingers of the waves as they washed onto the beach and quickly retreated to the ocean.

As they approach, he saw that they were a woman with two young children in tow. They were smiling and laughing as they neared him. The two boys were around the age of three and four, displaying the energetic qualities that all young toddlers have at that age. They jumped, ran, grabbed at each other, and tumbled onto the sand as one tried to get an advantage over the other. They laughed and looked to their mother for her approval as they raced to her open arms for a hug.

The woman also laughed, obviously loving the attention they adorned her with. Tucker could easily tell she truly enjoyed the playfulness of the boys as they walked along. This all brought a smile to his face.

The threesome was now at an angle where Tucker could clearly see the woman. She was lovely, with long, golden hair that shimmered in the sunlight and fell over her shoulders and down her back. The breeze caught her hair and blew it over her face. She gracefully pulled it away and continued on her stroll, following the boys as they circled her and ran past.

Tucker was totally immersed in the vision. The woman was beautiful. The long white summer dress she was wearing perfectly framed her figure and displayed the lines of an athletically toned body. There was something familiar about her that he could not put his finger on. She was attractive, yet Tucker did not have the masculine reaction he usually had when seeing such as beautiful woman. He was actually more intrigued by her and the boys' attire as they stopped to play. Their clothing was not what Tucker imagined someone would wear on such a splendid day at the beach. They appeared to be wearing knickers or some other fashion that was no longer in style. Regardless, the three were clearly enjoying their time together.

Their proximity had brought them adjacent to Tucker as he watched the dream unfold. The woman slowly turned her face in Tucker's direction, then pulled her hair back with one hand and smiled. Yes, smiled at him, with a familiar look in her eyes that quickly turned to terror as a dark covering of clouds approached.

She looked frantically for her boys as they slowly were engulfed by the incoming storm. With a look of despair, she raised her arms and turned back to Tucker. "*My boys?*" were the words she mouthed as the scene disappeared.

* * *

Tucker awoke with a start from his dream, feeling anguished yet alert. He sat up, stretched, and looked over at Karla curled up next to him. Her nude body was silhouetted under the single thin sheet as morning sunlight skated through the window shades, accentuating all her alluring curves.

Tucker was confused. For any stretch of beach in Central Brevard to have no one on it seemed extremely strange. But the dream, what did it mean? The vision of the woman as well as the children stuck in his mind. He no longer feared his dreams as he had when his Seminole ancestor, Osci, first entered them, and led him to the true identity of the skeleton found beneath the dune. No, this was different. He wanted to know more. He had had enough of them over the preceding months to know he shouldn't overlook them. He hoped for more dreams to reveal more information, which he knew they eventually would. Now the question still stuck in his head concerned the kids and that woman.

Who was she?

CHAPTER

4

The Lincoln Town Car slowly maneuvered the strips of speed bumps as it entered a quiet industrial area of Port Canaveral, Florida. The occupant in the back seat looked up from his report and peered at the driver with his usual scowl of annoyance.

"Be a little more careful," he commanded then turned his attention back to the document he was reading. The driver sank in his seat as he received the command from his boss.

The elderly gentleman was late as usual for his meeting, but his lateness was not accidental. It was more a message of his importance; to show he was in control of the situation. He thrived on firm control over any state of affairs and the intimidation of people. They could all wait, regardless of their titles, importance, or names. He was The Man, and he relished the role he played.

The car slowly maneuvered its way down a corridor between two steel warehouse buildings and came to rest among a collection of assorted vehicles underneath a palm tree that seemed out of place.

"Assholes," he murmured to himself. The use of chauffeured limos was not what the old man wanted to see parked outside the building in this industrial area of the port. They were all out of place. He had told them to be discreet, yet they had all traveled in a manner he knew drew unwanted attention.

With his cane in hand for the limp in his step, the elderly gentleman exited the car and approached a side door. A large man, eyes hidden behind sunglasses, smiled, said good morning, and politely opened the door for him.

With a slight limp, the head of this clandestine meeting made his way down the cold metal hallway and entered a makeshift conference room at the rear of the building.

All the expected attendees sat around a circular table, specifically selected so as not to distinguish a head guest. Many of the men sipped coffee and conversed in muffled tones.

"Good morning, everyone," the elderly gentleman started as he took his seat alongside a younger man. "I'm sure by this time everything is up to speed, as planned, and all of you have finished the work to secure the arrangements necessary to finalize our undertaking."

"Sir," began Jacob, a man small of stature, yet one of the most influential CEOs in the country, "we all have taken care of our responsibilities; I believe all necessary arrangements are moving toward completion."

The balding state senator from Tallahassee jumped in. "I'm happy to report that the I-95 widening project documentation is finalized, stamped, and complete. The work to widen below exit 191 will continue as planned. I just needed to make sure my constituents from that area would get the payback promised for their vote."

The man in charge nodded his head in acknowledgment and quickly looked at the man to his left for more information.

Davis stirred nervously and said, "As you all know, the port is now expanded, and we'll have all the facilities needed when our operation commences. There will also be enough land available to develop in the future as need be."

"Very good, gentlemen, everything appears to be moving along as planned. From my standpoint, the land we need will be in our possession within the month."

He looked in the direction of an individual who had been silent up to that point. "Speak up. I can see the question in your eyes."

"Well," the man from the county stammered. "I'm a little concerned about our security arrangements. If anything ever leaked out about our work and intentions…"

The old man cut Andrews off in a cold voice of authority. "We only have one month left, and after that, I'll be damned if I care about what others think, and neither should you." He smacked his cane on the floor in annoyance. "You will be richer than your wildest dreams. Now get a pair of balls and take control of yourself. We've worked too long and hard on this project to run scared or screw things up." The man of importance from Cocoa receiving the verbal berating slouched in his chair in embarrassment.

The old man quickly looked at the man they called J.T., who was from the company in charge of security for the site.

"Anything to report, J.T., which might calm the fears of our nervous counterpart?" the old man asked.

He responded confidently, "No, sir. Everything is protected at our location. The site is secure and waiting for the delivery of equipment."

"Are there any other concerns?" the old man asked as he rose from his seat with a thump of his cane on the floor. He waited another second, made eye contact with everyone in the room, and then said: "Remember, all communications are to be done by courier. No e-mails, text messages, or phone calls. Is that understood?" This was not a question, but a command that reverberated from the old man's throat. Everyone nodded in agreement as he leaned on his cane and ambled toward the exit door.

As he turned the corner, a smile came to his face. He thought to himself, *men of power my ass; they're nothing but weak-minded individuals, easily influence by money.* He loved this feeling of control, especially over self-proclaimed powerful men of government and industry—senators, representatives of government, and CEOs of major corporations.

All fools. It's amazing it took the country so long to fall into despair with these idiots in charge. Sometimes people don't know what's good for them; they have to be shown. When I get done with Brevard County, the rest of the country will be thanking me.

CHAPTER

5

As chief executive for the *Brevard Daily*, Mitch had a new hop in his step as he entered his office to answer a call. He felt good, and why shouldn't he? The paper was now solvent, or close to it. The publicity from Tucker's stories had generated enormous revenue and attention. The circulation of the paper had tripled and remained at that level for the past few months.

Who would have thought, Mitch smiled to himself, that Tucker Lee Anderson would be the new media sweetheart of Central Florida? Hell, if not the entire state. Tucker's eye-opening investigative reports into the growth of local corruption, from past to present, had shocked this quiet, sometimes pretentious community.

How Tucker came about his information was a heavily guarded secret—until now. Mitch had planned to let the secret out; well, at least a little leak of it. The very idea that a prominent figure, a corrupt one at that, had been brought to his knees because of a dream—yes, a dream—that a small town reporter had had was sure to attract more attention for the paper, as well as, of course, revenue.

Mitch stood at his desk and picked up the receiver to speak to his waiting caller.

"Mr. Rennington, this is Linda Greenwood from the *United States Globe*. Thank you for taking my call."

"Not a problem, Ms. Greenwood. I am…am more than happy to speak with you this morning," Mitch answered as his newfound self-esteem took over. "And please, just call me Mitch." He smiled.

"Thank you, Mitch, I'll only take a few minutes of your time. I've tried to contact Tucker Anderson for over a week now. I need to ask him to confirm or deny the story that his reporting comes from the assistance of dreams and voices from beyond."

Mitch smiled. The little anonymous blurb he'd posted on the Internet and sent to the *Globe* had at least caught someone's attention.

Ms. Greenwood went on, "Can you give us any insight into this? Our readers want to know."

The *U.S. Globe* was one of the biggest gossip magazines in the United States. Journalists commonly referred to it as a rag of semi-believable stories. Headlines ranged from two-headed aliens to a baboon that recited the Constitution. Taking the magazine as actual news was a little far-fetched, but it sold, and sold well. It dominated the newsstands as well as the Internet.

"No, Ms. Greenwood, I can't deny…" he paused on purpose to spike her interest, then continued, "…or confirm your inquiry. We at the *Daily* have very high ethical standards and only Mr. Anderson can answer your questions—if he chooses to. He's been on an extended vacation. I do expect him back shortly."

Ethical standards? Yeah, okay, Mitch thought to himself. The almighty dollar is my standard.

Ms. Greenwood continued, "Well, Mitch, this story has a lot of interest. We've been holding back on it for some time now, but our editors are now ready to run with it, as early as tomorrow, and let our readers know that Tucker Anderson relies on the paranormal to get his information."

Mitch smiled, trying not to reveal the pleasure in his voice. "Well, that's at your discretion. I'll be sure to have Tucker return your call for a more intense interview when he comes in, and because you've been so up front, I'll make sure there are no repercussions from anything you print."

Mitch took a seat as he placed the receiver back on its cradle. With a smile on his face he said out loud, "Run the story? Absolutely!" He hoped Tucker wouldn't get too upset with this latest turn of events, but why should he? They were teammates, and the team needed this play to go into overtime. *Win or lose,* Mitch thought, *the longer it's played out, the more money we make.*

CHAPTER 6

"Okay, let's see if I understand this correctly," said retired Colonel James Trout, the supervising manager of operations for World Wide Security Corporation, or WWSC as it was known among its clients. "You two boneheads located the squatter and, without my authority, took matters into your own hands? Is that what you're telling me?"

J.T. stared at his two silent subordinates with piercing eyes and continued, "Since when are you permitted to make decisions without my clearance and act on a fucking whim?" He spat as his voice rose with each syllable.

Jesus Rodriguez, the smaller of the two, answered. "Sir, we engaged the individual in question, surveyed the scene, and determined the need to eliminate." The larger, more muscular of the two men simply stared straight ahead while standing at ease.

Both men had been two of the colonel's most accomplished, mission-sensitive special operatives when all three were receiving paychecks from the United States government. It was only natural they would follow him to his new position at WWSC.

The men all looked at each other in silence. The soft hum of a generator providing power to the mobile command center was the only sound. In actuality, it was really more of a small recreational vehicle. The hot, humid weather outside didn't help the tension building inside this cubicle.

"Colonel," the larger man finally spoke. "Our target needed to be eliminated. This wasn't our usual group of teenagers running through the woods at night, looking for a place to drink and party, the ones we usually just scare away. This man was a definite threat to the security of our mission."

Mission, the colonel thought to himself. *I hate that fucking word. Mission my ass.* This was a job that could make him rich, something that the military could not do. *It's a job, that's it. Nothing I'm willing to sacrifice anything for.*

As the colonel spoke, he rubbed his temples with his forefingers. "Okay then." His voice lowered. "Did you dispose of the body and remove any traces of his death in the area?"

"Well, sir…kinda," one of the men answered honestly.

The colonel raised his eyebrows; darts shot out of his eyes as his blood pressure started to boil. He quickly reverted back to his irritated state.

"The target was removed to a location where the natural predators of the area will eradicate any remains," the larger man quickly added.

"Are you insinuating that gators will take care of your mess?" the colonel snapped back.

"Sir, with all due respect, in this type of terrain, climate, and with natural factors, the remains will decompose within forty-eight hours. His body will no longer be a recognizable threat."

Trout restrained himself for the moment and decided not to come down too hard on his men; he still required their assistance. Besides, they were not individuals you wanted to mess with, even from the colonel's standpoint. They were trained pit bulls that needed to be handled carefully.

"Okay, okay," the colonel answered as his voice lowered again. "I want the two of you to recon the squatter's cabin. Check to make sure he hasn't made notes about activity going on in the area or anything that can be linked to our existence." Both men nodded in agreement.

The colonel continued, "Now I'm sure I don't have to tell you to be discreet and leave nothing to chance, is that understood?" Again the two men nodded in unison.

"And the next time you think about doing something without my fucking approval, don't. Is that understood?"

Both men looked at each other, then back at the colonel. In that instant Trout swore he saw a smirk that sent a chill down his spine, but the two men now looking at him responded with, "Yes, sir."

"Okay then, go. Get the hell out of here and be careful," the colonel responded, wanting the conversation to end and the two loons out the door.

Trout needed to keep reminding himself that he had hired two of the best, but he knew they couldn't be trusted. The loyalty they had once vowed to him had been replaced with a dollar sign.

The humidity slapped the two subordinates in the face like a wet towel. "Fuck this place," Jesus said. "This shit hole is worse than our last assignment in Central America."

Both men looked at each other, shaded their eyes from the glare, smirked, and slowly made their way to their vehicles.

"Hey, at least back then you didn't see any fucking Indians running around the area chasing us."

Jesus answered, "I told you, it's only one Indian, and the damn thing seems to be following us."

"I'm telling you, it's the sun. It's getting to ya."

Picking up the rest of their gear, both men jumped on their quads, looked over the vast expanse of land, and made their way toward Drew Babcock's cabin.

From the distance, lost in the shimmering heat of the wetlands, an apparition of a lone Indian watched as the two men slowly drove away.

CHAPTER

7

Long before the white man came, the local Floridians lived off the land, cherished its natural resources, and had minimal contact with the outside world. Hunting, trapping, fishing, and trading provided them with every significant economic need.

Then the onset of the white man's expansion into the untamed land began to shrink the amount of privacy the Indians had and forever altered the future of the land called "The River of Grass."

The Seminole Indians consisted mainly of the Muscogee and Hitchiti from the Lower Creek. Together with the remains of the Yamasee, and later a large Negro element of runaway slaves, they were determined to live forever among the mangroves and scrub palms of Florida.

While under Spanish rule, the Seminole became involved in hostilities with the United States during the War of 1812. Later, during skirmishes in 1817 known as the first Seminole War, the highly proud Indians gained a reputation as ruthless and dangerous adversaries.

With a treaty in 1823, the Seminole ceded most of their lands to the United States, expecting in return a central reservation that never materialized. Through the years, plans were made to relocate the Seminole Nation off of the Florida Peninsula to remote areas of Oklahoma and Arkansas.

Under the leadership of the great Osceola, the remaining tribe retreated into the Everglades and surrounding swampland and prepared for battle. Thus began the second Seminole War of 1835, and again a later clash that erupted from 1856 to 1858. After the war, a small yet determined group found safe haven in the swamplands of the Everglades and surrounding area. These were the ancestors of today's Seminole Indians.

Out of war, men are born. One Seminole, though not nearly as well-known as Osceola, became the spiritual leader of the Seminole Nation, embodying the qualities of pride, defiance, and independence.

Abiaka had a dominant role during and after the leadership of Osceola. He was the one leader who remained in Florida and would not entertain the acceptance of a flag of truce. To this day, the Seminoles are the only tribe to have never signed a peace treaty with the United States.

During his time with Osceola, Abiaka took a bride and fathered a number of sons. To his disappointment, his oldest sons abandoned the Seminole way of life and relocated to villages of the white man.

Osci was Abiaka's youngest son, and during the calm periods between 1842 and 1856, Abiaka taught Osci to carry on the spiritual vows of his proud people.

Osci became immensely protective of his Seminole land and led a number of raids to remove intruders from the area. With the rumbling of war drums between the northern and southern United States, the attention shifted away from the Seminole and they were finally allowed to live quietly in the swamplands.

Abiaka was enormously proud of his son. The young Seminole never left his father's side and spent countless hours soaking up the knowledge his father presented him. Abiaka and Osci would leave for weeks at a time and traverse deep into the interior of the Everglades, where they became one with the land and where every nuance the land provided was implanted into the spirit of the young man.

Osci was taught how to hunt and survive off the natural resources of the land. On returning to his people, Osci and his proud father would bring venison, rabbit, alligator hides, and meat as well as baskets of salted fish.

Both were described as men of another world who could communicate with nature as well as the spirits of past great Seminole ancestors.

As Osci grew older, he was entrusted with being the keeper of the ancestral hunting ground. This land consisted of millions of acres that stretched from the Everglades, past the great lake, and farther north to the cape area known as the land of sea and dunes.

Osci would travel the land for weeks at a time and return only to meditate and connect with the spiritual leaders of the past.

On Abiaka's death, the twenty-three-year-old Seminole set out on a journey that would forever change his life.

As time does, the present slowly became the future, and Osci mysteriously vanished. Many rumors persisted about Osci's disappearance.

Legend has it that the handsome Seminole, with his muscular stature, tan skin, and long, black hair became involved with a white woman while her husband was away fighting in the great North-South War. Many said that they had a child together, but after that, no one seems to know.

Through Osci, the great bloodline of Abiaka lived on to the present day through the family of one Gladys Anderson and later her grandson, Tucker.

CHAPTER

8

Returning to work was not something I looked forward to, but nothing I dreaded either. Being a local celebrity again had its little perks and advantages—like my new parking space next to Mitch's and a real office, not just a cubicle hidden in the corner.

I swung my old Jeep Cherokee into the assigned spot adjacent to Mitch's and immediately noticed his new Cadillac STS V-Coupe. I have to admit, the automobile was impressive, and its shine just about blinded me as the morning sun reflected off the fender. I really thought that, after all the financial trouble the paper went through, Mitch would be more frugal with his money. But after the windfall of cash and attention the paper received from my articles, I could understand his temptation to splurge a little. As for me, the advantages of my hefty raise were nice. My old Jeep sufficed, and I actually had some savings set aside for a nice little condo beachside that I had been watching for a while.

I quickened my pace toward the building's entry foyer, hoping to reach the air-conditioned lobby before the humidity soaked through the back of my shirt. When I opened the door, a refreshing rush of cold air greeted me. I just missed the elevator, so I made my way to the stairwell, walking myself up to the second floor.

"Morning, Alice," I greeted our receptionist as I entered the suite of offices that made up the *Brevard Daily*.

Alice simply sat and smirked as I walked by. I was never one of her favorite people, and the fact that Claire had dumped me obviously had not helped to keep me in her good graces.

"Hey, welcome back, superstar," was Cliff's comment as he walked past me. He was one of our junior staff editors, and I smiled and slapped him on the ass as we passed. He just chuckled and continued on his way.

Then something unusual happened.

Applause!

A rousing greeting filled the air as people stood, clapped, and whistled as I made my way down the aisle of desks and cubicles.

What the hell was this all about?

This caught me off guard for a second, but then I figured everyone was still happy about my newfound notoriety and the attention I had brought the paper—or at least the little extra money I helped put in their pockets. They were just having some good old fun with me. What the heck, I could go along with that, so I waved, smiled, and blew a few kisses in the direction of the female staffers.

I continued to play along, but then caught Claire's gaze from the corner of my eye. The smirk on her face quickly turned into a laugh.

Did you ever see someone laugh and then realize they were laughing at you, not with you? That was the look I read on Claire's face as I passed. *Must be because our relationship ended badly*, was the thought that first hit me. *Oh well, can't win them all.*

I strolled down the hall and entered my new office. An old friend and colleague had retired just in time to open up this little corner of luxury for me. Still, the amenities were amazing: mahogany desk, fully stocked wet bar, new computer system, as well as a forty-two-inch plasma hanging on the wall. I sat in my high-backed leather chair and spun myself around like a kid at an ice cream parlor counter, stopping only to admire the view of the western portion of the property, which included an orange grove, outside my window.

"Ah, it's good to be the king," as Mel Brooks said in *History of the World Part One*, but what the hay.

Where to start? Ah, let's see now. I spun around and decided to check my voice mail. Leaning over and hitting the recall button immediately alerted me to forty-eight messages.

What the hell? I knew I garnered some attention, but damn… forty-eight?

Beep #1 – "Dad, I didn't call your cell 'cause I didn't want to disturb you on your vacation. I need a favor from you." It was my daughter, Jessie, sounding a little more chipper than usual. "I'm going to the prom with a senior. Oh my God, Daddy, he's so cute! You gotta meet him." She went on excitedly, "Mom said it'd be okay with you, and you and her would go halvsies on my dress. I know I can count on you, Daddy. Love ya."

Jessie totally caught me off guard. She was growing up way too fast for my liking, and now she's been asked to the prom? Shit, that was kind of hard for me to swallow, and being asked by a senior was not something I was excited about. I remembered my senior prom…oh man, and what I had planned. I needed to have a talk with her.

I listened to the next forty or so messages, which included requests for me to speak at the local Rotary luncheon, be interviewed by a number of reporters, and appear on the local morning show. I smiled and figured what the hell, time to give the folks a little taste of Tucker Lee Anderson.

Then I heard…*Beep.* "Hello, Mr. Anderson. My name is Martha Enland from Mims. I was hoping you could help me out. My little Pekinese named Sparky passed away last week, and I miss her terribly. I was wondering if you could contact her in the great beyond so I know she's okay."

What the fuck?

"I was reading the article about you in the *US Global* today and……"

An article about me? What article?

I cut off the message and listened to the next few. All were asking for some type of help contacting people from the vast beyond.

Then I noticed Cliff and his sidekick, Evan, standing at my door holding up a newspaper that headlined:

"Reporter Works From Beyond to Solve Crimes."

"Holy shit," I mouthed.

"Seems like your little secret's out," Cliff snickered. "You got some nice publicity here, my friend." He laughed as his head disappeared around the corner.

How…? I don't…?

Who could have known about my dreams? Only four people were privy to that information: Craig, Karla, Nan, and…MITCH! DAMN IT!

I bolted from my chair and shot to his office.

I raced past his secretary and entered his office, where Mitch turned and looked at me with a smile, the *US Global* in his hand.

"Hey, Tuck, hope your vacation was enjoyable. I've been very busy," Mitch said, clearly gloating over his latest publicity stunt.

CHAPTER
9

Pulling into the parking spot in front of my home, or should I say Mitch's palatial yacht, which I was living in, my mind was awash in thought. The changes in my life over the past few months could only be described as, to say the least, dramatic.

The discovery of my ancestor Osci and his child's skeleton, the revelation that we were actually related, and finding out that the murderer of the child was in the family lineage of one of the most powerful men in the state, was incredible. It was bad enough my long-estranged mother was married to the asshole, but finding out that my dreams had led me to them was strange as hell.

My recently deceased grandmother, who I'd called Nan and who had raised me after my father's boating accident—God rest their souls—had always told me that family, no matter how big, small, or distant, was the key to our being. Though she had left this life, we were still connected by spirit through time and space.

Now here I was, financially more secure from my investigative reports, my life finally in order, and enjoying a newfound respect as a journalist in my home town. Well, that was until this afternoon's embarrassment.

Mitch explained his reasons for the publicity stunt. I couldn't really agree with them, but he'd stuck with me over the years through thick and thin: my divorce, bad finances, and drinking, so what was I to do? As much as he owes me, I owe him. As he says, we're teammates, so this was not something I planned to argue.

I was still living on Mitch's yacht and loving every minute of it. But the time had now come to move on and make a lifestyle change. I was getting ready to purchase a little waterfront condo in Satellite Beach.

I exited my Jeep and began my slow march along the docks to my mooring when a familiar voice startled me from behind.

"Hey, stranger," came the voice of Doug, my slip mate. "Long time no see. You have a nice bit of R&R?"

I turned to greet him as he approached, flip-flops slapping his heels and two bags of groceries in his hands.

"It was great, Doug. I had one hell of a time." I smiled.

"I bet you did. I saw that little sweetie you went with, my boy. Nice pickings, son."

We both just laughed. Doug was quite a character. Though there was an age difference of about twenty years or more, we fast became friends after meeting at one of Mitch's earlier parties. Doug kept my head grounded and was a great source of confidence for me. He had sailed down from New Jersey years earlier after a messy divorce and just needed to get away from it all. Being an accomplished boatman, he sailed the Caribbean for a number of years, stopping at all the enchanted ports before mooring here in Melbourne. Other than that, I didn't know too much about him, except for the beer we both liked and the occasional cigar we smoked together.

I looked at him and smiled. "Yeah, she is a hottie. Kind of surprised she's with me."

"Don't sell yourself short, my boy," he answered. "You're a great catch for any lady."

A slight breeze blew as the sailboats rolled gently on the change of tide. Mast buckles clanged an echo across the marina, giving it a magical feel as the sky changed colors. The setting sun reflected an orange glow as it slowly set in the western sky.

"Red sky at morning, sailor take warning. Red sky at night, sailor's delight," Doug chimed in. "Say there, lad, I was gonna run up to the Texas Road House and grab some grub as well as a beer or two. Want to join me? My treat."

The sound of that perked up my ears. Plus, after the day I had, a good steak and a couple of beers sounded like a good idea right now.

"You know what, Doug, my old man, that sounds like a plan to me. Give me ten minutes to shower up and change these sweaty clothes and I'll be right with you."

Doug smiled. "See you in ten."

I went below deck, reached the forward cabin, selected my clothes, and jumped in the shower.

* * *

Doug looked around before quietly going below his forty-six-foot Lancer and sliding a safe box from under a hidden portside compartment. He removed a key from around his neck and opened it. After removing a package of papers, he found what he was looking for. Opening the leather-bound journal, Doug wrote the entry, "He's back, things progressing well." With a smile on his face he removed a print from the binding and looked at it for a moment before placing it back in its rightful place. He then locked everything securely back into a small, secret compartment built into the hull.

Finished with his report, Doug walked to the starboard porthole and watched for the emergence of Tucker as he had so many times before.

CHAPTER 10

Teenagers from Brevard County are no different from their counterparts in other areas of the country. They enjoy their freedom, especially out of eyesight from adults, and sampling the fruits of maturity along the way.

One place for these teens to gather is west of Interstate 95. From various towns, teens meet off the beaten path to experience the rites of passage to adulthood. As evening sets in, pickups as well as all other manner of vehicles find their way to this remote western portion of the county. Here they congregate in circles around campfires with radios blasting to drink, smoke, and party without the nagging that comes with adult supervision. Many dance as the shimmering light of the campfire casts shadows across the ground, giving an eerie feel to the reflections that bounce off the tailgates of the pickups.

Brought to the party by an older boyfriend, one such teenager was there for the first time tonight, relishing her newfound freedom. As she partied the night away under the stars, fifteen-year-old Jessie Anderson left her inhibitions behind and enjoyed the fruits of youth.

From a distance, two solitary souls stood atop a knoll in the watery marshland, watching the evening unfold in front of them through binoculars.

"Goddamn kids," remarked the larger of the two men, who was named Jack Prescott. "You'd think their fucking parents would like to know where the hell they all are tonight."

"They're just kids, Jack," said the smaller man with a smile. "Don't you remember what it was like when you were that age? Getting drunk and chasing tail? They're not bothering anyone."

Jack grimaced. "Yeah, I do remember, but we weren't in a high-security location. We have an area to keep secure, and these kids could compromise our mission. We're getting a hell of a lot of money, and I'm not blowing it over these punks."

"Well, what the hell would you like to do? Eliminate all of them?" the smaller man, named Jesus, said. "Wait, let me rephrase that. I know exactly what you'd like to do. Especially to the females."

Jack smiled.

Jesus went on, "Let's just sit here and wait and see what develops. There are about sixty kids over there, and if any roam too far from the site, we'll assess the situation, intercept, and access our options. These are local kids, Jack. They'll certainly be missed. Not like those kids with Texas tags on their car we eliminated a few weeks ago. No one will ever look for those two here."

Jack nodded in agreement and continued to monitor the party through his binoculars.

Jesus continued, "It was bad enough we wasted the old man last week. We don't need to take any more chances. Maybe we'll see a show or two as the night progresses. I've already seen some of the girls drop their tops as they hump and grind to the music. Just sit back and enjoy."

Jack stood quietly and half listened to what his associate was saying. "Yeah, the old man was no big deal. We had him under surveillance for over a month, and not one fucking person even gave a shit about him. Taking him out was a given. We didn't need him getting any closer to the Zone. The gators and vultures have probably had a nice feast by now." Jack laughed.

Jesus just looked at Jack. *What a weird fuck he is* ran through his mind. *He's the best at what he does, but DAMN!*

A light, cooling breeze rippled across the wasteland as the evening became darker. Both men fell silent and continued with their surveillance.

Shit, I can't believe I have to take orders from this little shit, the larger man thought. *The entire operation could go up in flames if we screw this up. They all need to grow a set of balls, and then we'd be in better shape.*

The men stood their guard and watched with curious eyes as the festivities slipped deep into the night. Below their little knoll, an alligator lurked, watching them with glowing eyes.

CHAPTER

11

The beer was cold, food outstanding, and the waitress as pretty as ever. A good night or, better yet, a great night was unfolding, putting a nice end on my otherwise bizarre day.

A six-ounce sirloin cooked to perfection for Doug and the smothered chicken for me was just what the doctor ordered.

With his mouth full, Doug still continued to weave his tales as I sat mesmerized.

"Tell ya what, my son. You haven't lived until you've spent time on the high seas getting to know yourself...and any pretty little thing that wants to sail with you." He laughed after taking a guzzle of his beer.

Doug was one hell of a storyteller. My problem being I couldn't tell if it was all bullshit. Nevertheless, he had some of the best stories I had ever heard. His dark, tanned features, weathered face showing the crow's feet of time, as well as his salt and pepper hair, gave him a handsome look of distinction. Kind of what I thought I might look like someday…if I was lucky.

"Excuse me, darlin'," he said to the waitress. "You just keep these here beers ice cold and comin', and there'll be a little something extra in it for you at the end of the night," he said as he gave the waitress a wink.

To my surprise the waitress returned the wink and said, "I'll be looking forward to it, handsome."

I was shocked by that one, to say the least. I know the girls are working for tips, but damn, she was about thirty years younger than Doug and pretty as anything. I couldn't get a response like that from a woman if I begged.

Seeing my reaction, he smiled and went on, "The time I spent in Barbados was a memorable one. I met this little twenty-eight-year-old filly, and she wanted to join my crew for the sail up to St. Thomas."

"What?" I said. "You had a crew?"

"Yes, I did, yes, I did," he said after another beer was delivered with a big smile from the waitress. "She was my crew. She kept me shipshape…if you know what I mean."

I'm afraid I did know what he meant and just sat dumbfounded as he slapped me on the back.

"Doug, you don't mean …"

"Yes, I do. She kept the old ship's mast at a full run."

I sat back, took a good look at him as I sipped my beer. He was an older man, about twenty years older than me, handsome and in great shape. But to get girls…or should I say women more than half his age…into the sack was truly unbelievable.

"Son, if you never moored at the base of the Pitons in St. Lucia, woke to the light reflecting off its summit, dived bare ass for your morning lobster with a gorgeous young female, well, you haven't lived."

I smiled. "Damn, Doug, that's every man's dream. For you to pull that off is awesome. But she was twenty-eight years old? Now that's, that's…" I didn't know what to say.

"Yeah, she is, or should I say was, a sweet thing. She's thirty-two now. She clung to me like a barnacle, but I didn't need that type of emotional connection at my age."

I watched as the waitress approached, ignored me, and brought two new beers over while smiling at Doug. "These are on me," she said with a smile as she slipped him her number.

What the fuck?

"If you don't mind me asking, how the hell old are you anyway?

He looked at me and smiled. "Take a guess."

He sat up straight, gave me a goofy smile, and finally laughed as I began to speak.

"Okay, let's see here. After your divorce up in New Jersey you sail to Bermuda and then to Barbados. You hang there for a while and make your way through the islands with a few hotties to keep you company and end up here in Melbourne. So I'll say you're fifty."

He just smiled and pointed to the ceiling.

"Fifty-six," I said.

Again he just pointed skyward.

"Higher? No way. You can't be sixty! Can you?"

I was forty-two…okay, turning forty-three, and this guy looked good, if not better than me.

"Don't even say you're near seventy."

"No, lad," he said with a smile as his nose crinkled up and he sat back to let our surroundings set in. "Let's just say I haven't reached that port yet, but the dock isn't that far away. I'm sixty-seven."

I almost fell out of my seat with his admission. The man was now my idol. I raised a glass and made a toast. "Doug, to a long life, full sails, a fair wind, and a large bottle of Viagra."

We both laughed until he became solemn and just smiled at me.

After all was said and done, Doug paid the bill as promised, objected to my offering any compensation, and got up to leave. Our waitress approached and gave a curt good-bye to me and a long hug and kiss for Doug.

"You old dog you," I started. "You knew her all the time and didn't tell me."

"I don't know her, lad, but if I'm lucky, I'll know her a little better in the next few days." He smiled. "Son, I just love the females, and they just seem to love me too."

He must really like me to keep calling me son. But what the fuck? I can't believe this. What the heck am I? Chicken shit? He has some animal magnetism or something.

We both stumbled out the door and headed west toward the bridge and our marina.

* * *

A lone customer sat in the corner of the bar as he had for the past three hours, nursing his drink. The irate bartender gave him a sneer as he threw two dollars on the bar for a tip.

"Yeah, they're together," he said into his cell phone. "No, nothing'. They just ate, drank, and acted like two school kids. I'll follow them and report later. No, I don't think the Tucker character has any idea who he is and what's going on. I'll keep an eye out."

The stranger stayed far enough behind so as not to be noticed as he followed the two men back to their marina.

CHAPTER 12

Tucker once again found himself on a dune overlooking the emerald-green ocean, but this time, a low covering of dark, ominous clouds shaded the sun.

Things were different from his last dream. A feeling of dread washed over him. Tucker looked around but saw no one. A feeling of panic came over him until he saw a woman come into view.

The woman approached alone, head down but for an occasional glance at the sea. She was an older woman, and Tucker suddenly recognized her as the same woman from his earlier dream. Her beauty still radiated: long, flowing hair and a gracefulness that only a few can achieve. However, her smile was gone, and she walked at a slower, more deliberate pace.

She was not followed by children as before. No, she was totally alone. She stopped and sat on the edge of the sand, pulling her knees to her chest as she stared at the sea. Even though a soft wind tossed her hair about, she made no attempt to brush it away from her face.

Lightning started to flicker over the ocean, and the once calm sea became awash in long, rolling waves, quickly turning into white caps as they crashed on the shallow reef of coquina.

Tucker drifted toward the woman as if a magnet pulled him closer. He paused as the woman finally pushed the hair from her face, and her tear-laden eyes locked on Tucker's.

He froze. The woman looked so familiar to him, yet he could not make out who she was. Lightning continued flashing as the woman slowly stood and raised her arms toward Tucker. Her lips parted as she tried to get him to understand her request. Flashes continued to silhouette her, but the incessant thunder and crashing sea drowned her words. Still she continued to speak until Tucker finally understood: "Help, it's me."

With a start, I was sitting up in bed. *Holy shit,* I thought to myself as the boat rocked from side to side in a late night storm. *What the fuck is going on? It can't be happening again.*

I sat for a moment with my head in my hands, letting my mind clear. My head ached from the beer that Doug and I had consumed at the roadhouse. I looked at my alarm clock and saw 2:22 a.m. illuminated in the darkness. Shit, that always seemed to be the time I had one of these dreams.

Rousing myself from bed and making my way to the galley, I grabbed a bottle of water, sipped it, looking out the porthole to view the marina and boats as they rolled in their slips. Doug's cabin light was still on, as where a few other vessels'. I continued to struggle with my dream.

Damn, thought I was done with this. At least my Seminole ancestor, Osci, wasn't in it scaring the crap out of me like before. But the woman...who was she, and where did her boys go?

I sat for a second and cleared my mind before making my way to the master cabin. Sitting down on the edge of the bed, I felt a chill run down my spine as I finally realized who the woman was.

No, it couldn't be. But why were there two boys?

As I lay back down, it became clearer. I now realized who the woman was. But why she was asking for help still wasn't clear.

CHAPTER

13

"Good morning, Tucker," came the voice I had learned to loathe over the years as I raised my cell phone to my aching head. It was my ex-wife, Marion, not the first voice I wanted to hear as I suffered through my first hangover in years.

"Oh, hi, Marion," I answered. "What gets you up so early in the morning to call me?"

"Morning? Yeah, okay, Tucker, let's try one in the afternoon, you los…" I pulled the phone away from my aching head as she snarled in my ear, knowing what she was finishing her sentence with. I learned a while ago that her vitriol was not worth getting upset over.

One in the afternoon? No way, I thought as I sat up to catch my bearings and look over to find my alarm clock resting on the floor.

"Shit, my alarm never went off," I unconsciously said out loud.

"More like you hit the snooze button one too many times this morning," came the voice from my phone. "I bet the thing's on the floor and across the room from you throwing it while you were drunk."

Damn, she knows me way too well.

I slowly rose to my feet and stumbled into the galley to fix myself a cup of coffee, listening to her as she ranted and raved about the kids and a number of other things that didn't concern me.

I reached the counter and was surprised to find a Starbucks container and a note from Doug: "Here you go, my boy. I took the liberty of picking you up a little 'waker-upper' after the night you had. Doug."

What's with the "my boy" shit anyway, I thought, picking up the now cold coffee and placing it in the microwave before turning my attention back to my crazed ex-wife.

"So, Marion, as I said, what gives me the honor of getting your call so early…this afternoon? I know my child support is on time, 'cause it's now garnished from my paycheck. So what can you do me out of this time?"

"Very funny, Tucker, your payments are fine…for now. I'm sure they'll be late again once that rag you work for goes under or dumps your ass. Do you even work anymore?" She laughed sarcastically.

"Well, sweetheart," I continued sarcastically just to piss her off, "stardom does have its privileges." Though I didn't believe I was a star of any type, I knew the comment would get to her.

I continued, "Since I broke those stories I have a lot of leeway now to write as I want. I still have the sports page, and if you haven't noticed, my own column now runs weekly. Mitch owes me for helping the paper out."

Marion laughed. "Stardom? Yeah, okay. I saw the *Globe* headlines. Nice article they ran on you about ghosts and spirits helping you." She made some goofy ghost noises into the phone. "Who have you talked too lately? Uncle Robert E. Lee, that Indian uncle of yours, or one of your other horse-stealing relatives?"

Ouch. That was a low blow. She was witty and had a smart-ass remark for everything I said, but again, she wasn't worth getting into a pissing contest with.

"Well, you sound happy as usual, Marion. Let's forget the chit-chat and cut to the chase," I said, removing my hot coffee from the microwave.

The rich aroma, lifted by the gentle crossing breeze coming through the porthole, filled the cabin as our conversation continued.

"You owe me a check, Tucker, for the gown."

"Gown, what gown are you talking about?"

"Jessie's prom dress. You promised her you'd pay half. You're not sticking me with the entire bill."

We had had our few months of truce during the time I was gaining all my notoriety, but now she was back to normal.

"Oh yeah, sure, no problem. Just tell me what the damage is and I'll write you out a check."

"I'd rather have cash from you," she answered.

"No, Marion, I'll write a check. Take it or leave it." Boy, am I tough or what?

"Yeah, okay. Three hundred and ninety-eight dollars, to be exact."

"Fine, Marion, I'll cut you a check for half, one ninety five, and give it to Jess —"

She cut me off with a giggle. "Hold on, champ. That's three hundred and ninety...each."

I almost choked on my coffee.

"What, the dress cost seven hundred and eighty bucks? Holy shit, Marion. Who's she going to the prom with, the Prince of Windsor?"

She laughed again. "No, wise guy, just a very nice young man from a prominent family up in Cocoa."

Now I cut her off. "That's another thing I wanted to talk to you about. What made you decide to let our fifteen-year-old daughter go to the prom at her age anyway?"

Marion didn't have to answer. When I heard the words "prominent family", I knew that "image" was the only thing my ex was concerned about. So pimping my daughter out with this kid was something she didn't even give a second thought to. What a bitch.

"Well, Tucker, if you must know, his daddy is a friend of Charles's. He's one of the best neurosurgeons on the East Coast. He and Charles are major contributors to the new hospital in Viera," she said smugly.

Wonderful, she still shakes me down for every penny and her husband is a doctor and a major player in a new hospital.

"Anyway, Tucker, Jess will stop by and pick up the money...I mean your rubber check. I would love to just talk to you," she said and laughed again, "but some of us are working people and have things to do. Ciao."

She was gone in an instant. Still the ever-loving bitch. Job my ass. She wouldn't know work if it hit her in the face. I hung up my phone.

I picked up my coffee, took a few sips, and headed topside.

Hopefully the fresh air would help clear my headache.

I stepped on deck and ran smack into Jessie as she came aboard.

CHAPTER
14

"I know, sir. Yes, I understand completely. The area is secure and everything is moving along as planned. Yes, sir, I realize that. I'll meet you at the staging area at eighteen hundred. My men will be stationed at various intervals. Thank you, sir. I'll see you then."

Colonel Trout hung up his secure satellite connection and slowly rose from behind his desk. His head ached from the migraine that had been racking his brain for the past week.

He headed slowly to the small kitchenette at the rear of the command center. Filling a cup with water from a cooler, he reached into the cupboard and shook out a number of Advil, which were quickly swallowed.

The phone call had been expected. He had no problem updating his superiors about Area 176's security. He did, however, have a problem reporting the death of the squatter, thinking it was better left unsaid.

He stood at the window and let his mind empty as he gazed out over the forsaken expanse of land.

"I wonder what those two nitwits, Jesus and Jack, are up to right now?" he murmured to himself, hoping they weren't doing anything that could cause problems. "All they have to do is keep any stragglers away from the area. How hard can that be?" he wondered out loud. *Damn,* he thought, *better not jinx myself.*

The heat and bugs alone were good enough to deter most people from ignoring the "No Trespassing" signs. The kids that showed up to party on weekends were the only occasional problem. But he had to agree with the naturalist; there was a quiet beauty to the immense piece of land. A mixture of scrub pines and palms broke up the landscape at various intervals. The tall grass swayed, and the heat gave the mirage of shimmering water as it rose into the air.

He took another sip of water and started to feel his headache subside. The colonel smiled at the realization that this mission would make him rich. If things went as planned, he'd be in charge of security for one of the biggest and most lucrative projects to ever hit the United States.

I guess I better contact Jesus and Jack and make sure they're around when the suits show up. Always good to have a show of force on hand when the boss arrives.

CHAPTER
15

With long, flowing blond hair, sun-kissed skin, a beautiful turquoise sundress and heels, Jessie wrapped her arms around me for a tight hug.

"Hi, Daddy," she squealed as I gave her a kiss on the cheek and pushed her an arm's distance away to make sure this beautiful girl...no, let's say young woman...was really my fifteen-year-old daughter.

"Hi, honey," I answered. "You're here early. Shouldn't you be in school right now? And how did you get here?"

She laughed. "Oh, Daddy, you're so silly. School has been out for a while, and I'd like you to meet my boyfriend, Wayne."

Wayne? Who the hell is Wayne? I thought. I turned and looked down the dock and almost choked on my coffee as I saw who...no, let's say what...was walking my way.

You've got to be kidding me.

I looked from this…Wayne back to my daughter and was shocked at the puppy dog look I saw in her eyes as *this thing* approached.

I couldn't believe what I saw coming on board. Did this kid have a pair of pants that didn't hang off his ass? This was not the type of kid I expected my daughter to like.

"Daddy, this is Wayne. Wayne, this is my daddy."

The kid stepped over and shook my hand straight, sideways, gave me a half hug. Then he pounded his chest and gave me some sort of sign before saying, "Hey, dude, what's shaking?"

What the….dude? Shaking? Oh, this could turn ugly very quickly.

I took a long look at this…I don't know what to call him, but with his baseball cap on sideways and gold chains weighing down his neck, I just thought…thug.

Because of the goo-goo eyes my daughter was making, I decided to remain calm. I noticed Doug, now standing on his deck, had a grin that went ear to ear as he took in the scene unfolding in front of him.

I muttered, "Hello, Wayne. How are you?"

"Cool man, just cool. Love your crib you got here," he said as he looked around and tilted his body to one side while standing at an angle.

Is there something wrong with his leg that makes him stand like that? And crib. What the fuck is he talking about? A baby's crib?

I saw Doug take a seat on his boat with his full attention turned in our direction.

"Thanks," I replied. Even though I had no idea what he was saying. I looked at my daughter, who just smiled and followed her… shit, boyfriend as he walked around the boat.

I finally got her attention. "So, Jess, this dress you got, pretty nice I'm guessing from the price your mom told me?" I really wanted to double check the price, since I didn't trust her mother as far as I could throw her.

"Oh, I don't know, Daddy. It's hot and all. I guess it cost a lot, but I really didn't look at the price tag," she said as her gaze traveled back to Wes…Wayne. Damn it. I really wanted to hear the price again, and "didn't look at the price tag" sounded just like her mother.

"I'll go below and get you a check, hon, and don't let Wes fall overboard."

"It's Wayne, dawg. My name is Wayne," the kid answered.

Whatever. "Would you like anything to drink…Wes…Wayne?"

"No thanks, dude. I'm cool."

Cool…shit.

When I returned, I was more than surprised at what I saw.

There was Doug, now standing on my boat, laughing and joking with Jessie and Wes…Wayne. He and the kid were talking in some gibberish I didn't even understand.

"Here, honey," I said as I approached and whacked my head on the mainsail. I rubbed my head and handed her the check. "Make sure your mom gets that, okay?"

All three paused and smiled.

"You okay there, son?" Doug asked with a smile.

What's with the son shit again?

"Yeah, I'm okay. I see you already met my slip mate, Doug. Jess and Wes, this is Doug."

"The name is Wayne, man. That's my name," the kid said as he looked at me in annoyance.

"Thanks, Daddy," Jessie said as she leaned over to give me a kiss. "Isn't Wayne a dream?" she said, grabbing Wayne's hand and stepping off the deck down to the dock. "Make sure you're available in a few weeks to see us leave for the prom."

Dream? More like a fucking nightmare.

"Wouldn't miss it for the world, honey, and Wes, you stay cool now and be careful."

I heard the kid mumble something about his name as they both disappeared down the dock. Doug and I just stood there and watched as the two teens departed.

"What are you smiling at?" I snapped at Doug as he placed a hand on my shoulder.

He turned and faced me with the biggest shit-eating grin I had ever seen. "Your daughter, Jessie, is really a beautiful girl, lad. But that kid…" He started to laugh uncontrollably.

"It's not funny," I started, but his laugh was infectious and my smile broke into a chuckle. "No shit, I know she's gorgeous, but she's only fifteen. Say, by the way, what the hell were you and that kid saying to each other?"

"Remember, my boy, I've been around the block a few times, and even at my age I've picked up some of today's lingo. Don't forget I'm from Jersey, and I'm used to hearing that shit." He laughed again as I just shook my head.

Doug's mood suddenly turned serious. "Make sure you take care of that little girl, Tucker. They only come along once in a lifetime. Family is everything, no matter how much time separates them."

Wow, that must be a familiar saying. I'd heard that before.

"Yeah, I know," I answered. "My nana said the same thing, God rest her soul."

"Well then, I'm sure she must have been one hell of a woman."

"Yes, she was," I murmured as a new voice woke me out of my temporary trance.

"Ahoy there, Tucker! I just passed Jessie and some punk kid. She gave Uncle Craig a nice hug, but boy, are you in trouble with that piece of work she's with. I actually did a double take when she

60

said hello, she looks like she's twenty-one, if not a day," shouted my best friend, Craig, as he approached.

"Come on now. Enough of that crap already. You guys are giving me a freaking heart attack."

Craig came aboard, and I introduced him to Doug who immediately excused himself, mentioning something about running some errands.

"Craig, please give me a break on this. I'm a nervous wreck about Jessie. She's growing up so fast."

Craig laughed. "I'm just busting on you. I can remember when Carolyn started dating, I was a basket case. I actually had a few of the guys follow her and run background checks on them."

"Background checks? That's not a bad idea. When you get back to the station could you run that kid for me?"

"Sure, Tuck, I'm one step ahead of you. I got the tag number off the new little Beamer he was driving as they pulled away."

"Beamer? That figures. Fucking Marion, she's killing me with this high society thing. Hey, what the heck you doing down here anyway?"

"Oh, I was at some bullshit task force meeting over at Florida Institute of Technology, so I figured I'd kill two birds with one stone and see if you wanted to grab a lunch up at PJ's."

"Lunch? More like breakfast for me," I said with a laugh and went on, "I'll make an exception this time, but how about we hit Meg O'Malley's instead? I haven't been there in a while."

"Okay, sounds good to me. A few beers and a Cuban corned beef on rye might just make my day," came the answer from Craig.

We both laughed as I headed below to change my clothes.

* * *

Doug sat at his navigation station and peered out the porthole at Tucker as he had so many times before.

He liked Jessie and thought Tucker had one hell of a daughter, but he wasn't thrilled about the detective friend, Craig. He'd deal with him—at another time and place.

CHAPTER 16

Two large tractor trailers sat to the side of Route 532 just a stone's throw away from the intersection of Highway 520. Accompanied by two Hummer SUVs with dark, tinted windows, the caravan stood disregarded by other motorists on this seldom traveled Central Florida highway.

The group of people inside them knew they needed to get moving before the afternoon storm from the west blew in. Large thunderheads loomed in the distance, momentarily held at bay by the sea breeze emanating from the Atlantic. Dark streaks in the distant sky showed rain squalls falling erratically across the barren landscape.

"Where the hell are they?" came a voice from the rear passenger seat of the lead Hummer.

"They're on their way, sir. They'll be here in a minute," answered the driver's companion. "We're a little early and—"

The old man in the rear of the SUV cut him off. "If I want your fucking update about the time, I'll ask for it. Got it?"

"Yes, sir," the startled young man answered meekly while the driver cringed at the voice directed toward his partner.

Dusk had started to settle in, and the semblance of any traffic on the lonely stretch of highway was now nonexistent.

Two Land Rovers emerged from a large mix of overgrown foliage, one of them driven by Colonel Trout, the head security officer for WWSC. The gravel road it emerged from couldn't be seen by the unknowing eye. There were many entry points one could use to access Area 176, but this was the route chosen by the company's engineers. It had the proper foundation to handle the heavy traffic, and if everything went as planned, it would be turned into a new four-lane highway soon.

The colonel's Land Rover blinked its lights and swung around in front of the waiting caravan while the other SUV took up its position at the rear.

As lightning streaked the sky, the once impressive sight of two semis and a group of support vehicles ceased to exist. They had disappeared from the roadside, heading to a staging area five miles deep into the brush.

CHAPTER

17

"Are you sure about him, Tucker?" was the detective-like question from my childhood best friend, Craig. "I mean Doug? How much do you really know about this guy?"

Craig was always looking out for me. We'd been inseparable since elementary school. Over the years, we had leaned on each other for support in good times and bad. We were brothers in every sense of the word and couldn't have been any closer if genealogy had played a part.

He was my strength. From a five-year-old with no mother, to the boating accident death of my father when I was a teen, and now after my messy divorce, Craig had my back.

I also had his as well. His parents' divorce had devastated him when he was twelve, and the failure of not two but three marriages gave me reason to make sure he always landed on his feet, and he did. We both did. Craig had risen through the ranks of the sheriff's department to the top of the detective bureau. I had also landed on my feet and was now finally comfortable in my role as a local reporter.

"Yeah, Craig, I think I do. There's just a familiarity about the old geezer that I can't shake. He's a cool guy."

Craig just sat and stared ahead, finally looking at me only when our waitress brought over our orders.

"I don't know. I just can't get a feel for the guy. Maybe it's just my intuition kicking in, but something just doesn't sit right with me." Craig reached for his corned beef and rye and took a bite.

"Maybe so," I said. "He always has a smile on his face and makes me feel at ease. He's just a great guy to talk to."

Craig listened, sitting deep in thought, shrugging his shoulders as he continued to munch on his sandwich.

My cell chimed its familiar tune as I finished a swig of beer. Looking at the caller ID, I saw it was Karla.

"Hey, hon, glad you called. I was just thinking about you."

This brought a sudden reaction from Craig as he pretended to choke on his beer and raise his eyebrows toward his balding head, giving me the finger all at the same time.

"Sure, we'll take a look at the condo tomorrow. Of course I want you to come along. The real estate agent, Kathy Hile, said she'd call with my walk-through time in the morning. Okay, that sounds great...No, I'm with someone. Don't make me say that now. You know I do."

I looked at Craig smirking at me as if we were back in grade school. I gave him the finger in return.

Craig now wrapped his arms around himself and puckered his lips at me. A group of women having lunch at the next table looked over and giggled at his antics.

"Karla...yes, I do. No, I'm not afraid to say it. Okay, love you too...kitten, bye."

I hung up the cell and tried not to look at Craig.

"Kitten? Are you freaking kidding me? Kitten?" He laughed and almost fell out of our booth. "Haven't you learned anything from me after all these years?"

"You?" I snickered. "Oh, you're not exactly the best role model for anyone when it comes to women. How many times you been married?"

Craig winced and grabbed at his chest. "That one got me. Like a dagger through the heart, but no offense taken."

I smiled. "None given."

Craig suddenly went back to blowing kisses at me.

"Okay, I get it."

Craig started, "Wow, Tuck, seriously, I haven't seen you like this in a long time. She has you hooked. I haven't heard you say the L word to a woman and actually mean it in a long time. Good for you, buddy."

"I...I...she is something special. I haven't felt this way in such a long time about anybody. I feel like I'm a teenager again."

Craig smiled. "Good for you, Tuck, I'm happy for ya. You deserve a break."

We both grabbed our beers and toasted to our future good fortune as I continued, "Yeah, I hope so. It's taken some time, but I finally sense things might be looking up for me."

We finished our meals, paid our bill, and stepped outside as dusk slowly edged its shadow along the street of downtown Melbourne. There we shook hands and said we'd talk again in a day or two.

"I'll run a check on Wes...I mean Wayne, Jessie's boyfriend," Craig said with a laugh as we went our separate ways.

I walked down the block toward my Jeep, and all of a sudden an eerie feeling came over me. I turned and looked at the people milling around the sidewalks as they passed by.

Then I noticed a man. He caught my attention while looking at me through the crowd. Suspicion crept over me. Our eyes met, and he immediately turned away, stepping into a government-plated vehicle that whisked him away.

CHAPTER

18

In the distance, a lone sailboat with billowing sails glided quietly down the Indian River on its weekly journey, sails at full flow, a small wake in its trail, and a man standing at the helm, directing the boat on its course.

A little boy, Tucker, took a break from the playground, shaded his eyes, and walked to the river's edge to catch a glimpse of the boat. To his right, a group of friends played and joked with each other as the morning sun tickled the dew from the palms. Tucker waved in hopes of catching the attention of the man at the helm.

The explosion that followed a moment later resonated across the Space Coast. A ball of red and yellow flames reached high into the sky as the remnants of the boat scattered over the river's surface. Black smoke and the skeleton of the boat were the only reminders of the once sleek vessel.

Tucker watched intently, unsure of the spectacle unfolding in front of him. A young child named Craig came to Tucker's side and held his friend up as his legs started to tremble. An older woman came to Tucker's aid and whisked him away before the screams of "Daddy!" could emanate from his mouth.

The woman carried Tucker and whispered "*My boys*" as she raced from the area shielding the little boy from the tragedy on the river.

* * *

I awoke in a sweat, heart pounding as I sat up and looked at the alarm clock's time of 2:22 illuminated in the darkness.

Perspiration erupted from every pore of my body. I was soaked.

Oh my God, I thought, rising from the berth and leaving the cabin without waking Karla.

Making my way to the galley, I bent over the sink and filled my cupped palms with water, splashed my face, and rubbed the water across the back of my neck. I squeezed my eyes shut in hopes of removing the vision that now lingered in my consciousness of the explosion I had witnessed some thirty years ago. The feeling that overwhelmed me wracked my body as my heart continued to race. Tears welled in my eyes as the pain of losing my dad returned.

The memory was not one I wanted to relive. I had thought of that day many times, and visualizing it again was not something I wanted to experience now.

I sat down and was staring into space when Karla walked in. "Tucker, are you okay?" she said as she sat next to me and held my hand.

"I think so. It was just a dream, hon, but it was so real."

"Do you want to tell me about it?"

I looked into her eyes and nodded. For the first time in years I had someone I could talk to.

"Karla, it was so real. It was the day I saw my daddy die. I saw it all again, the explosion and everything. I could smell the smoke and feel the terror."

"Oh my God," she remarked. "I'm so sorry, honey."

She rubbed my back and wrapped her arm around me.

"That's not the only thing," I went on. "You know the woman in my other dreams that I didn't recognize? I didn't tell you before, but it's my nan."

CHAPTER 19

A number of years after the conclusion of the Civil War, a young entrepreneur from Ohio made his way to Jacksonville, Florida, for the winter of 1876. What started out as a retreat for his ailing wife quickly turned into a vision that would forever change the landscape of this land called Florida.

Henry Morrison Flagler fell in love with the climate and topography of this pristine area. He envisioned the endless possibilities the strangely unique peninsula offered. With its abundant land, he had the nerve to do what no one else dared: build a railroad through the sand and underbrush.

Returning to his beloved Florida in 1885, Flagler settled in Saint Augustine and purchased a number of short line railroads that would later be known as Florida's East Coast Railway. A few years later, Henry expanded his holdings and built a railroad across the

St. John's River, gaining access to the southern portion of the state. Thus began the race to create America's winter retreat. With his line snaking along the Indian River, small towns such as Titusville emerged and thrived from the railroad that headed to West Palm Beach and, years later, to the Keys.

By 1896 the opening of a new frontier had led thousands upon thousands of people to discover and claim their fortunes.

One such individual was Titusville native Hawthorn C. Groves. Hawthorn, with a lineage to the area, had the foresight to see the numerous opportunities investing in the land could bring. He quickly became one of the earliest real estate speculators in the state. In conjunction with a number of beneficiaries, Hawthorn bought over one million three-quarter acres of Central Florida real estate for pennies on the dollar. Much of the land was in the interior of the state, just west of the Indian River. He would have bought more land farther south if it were not for the quick thinking of one Barron Gift Collier, who became the biggest real estate tycoon Southern Florida had ever seen.

As time passed, the expansion that Southern Florida experienced never materialized for Hawthorn and his purchase farther north. On his death in 1939, the vast amount of land, at that time considered useless, remained part of the family's holdings.

At the young age of twenty-one, Gladys Anderson, Tucker Lee's nana, and Hawthorn's granddaughter, became heir of the vast wasteland. Her husband, William, handled the family holdings. In ensuing years he befriended two young attorneys to help with the proper paperwork needed to secure the family estate.

As time passed, one of the young attorneys became the most powerful political figure in Florida, whose illegal activities and past digressions would be uncovered by a small-time reporter named

Tucker Lee Anderson. With his investigative reporting, Tucker brought the politician to his knees, reporting a cover-up that had lasted for over a hundred years, revolving around the discovery of a child's skeleton beneath the dune.

CHAPTER
20

I wasn't able to fall back asleep after revisiting the sailboat explosion through my dreams. Karla slept peacefully next to me, snuggled up with a pillow between her legs and another held tightly to her chest. I continued to check the clock; time seemed to be moving at a turtle's crawl. At five thirty, it was time to get up.

Hoping not to wake Karla, I ran the bathroom faucet lightly, just enough to brush my teeth and wash my face. I pulled on my shorts and a sweatshirt for the morning chill then grabbed my sneakers and headed topside. Sitting for a second to lace up my sneakers, I marveled at the colors the early morning light brought to the new day while the sky brightened.

Walking from the yacht past Doug's boat, I noticed his cabin light was still on. Must be up early, I thought, or fallen asleep with the lights on. Nothing really unusual about it, but since he was a big advocate of going "green," I made a mental note to bust him about wasting energy.

I exited the marina and started my mile jog east toward the beach. Eau Gallie was just coming to life with early morning commuters heading to their mainland jobs.

The purpose of my jog was two-fold. First, I needed to clear the cobwebs out of my head before heading over to the office, making some sense of my latest dreams. Secondly, I wanted to check the surf. If it looked to be holding up, an afternoon surf session with my son Carl would be a good idea after I did my condo walk-through.

Carl was only nine, but the surf bug had bitten him. Something my ex-wife never wanted to happen, so the thought of him taking after dear old dad brought a smile to my face.

I made Canova Park in good time and walked up to the dune crossing, happy to see the azure sea as the sun sparkled in golden gleams of light across the water. The ocean was a sheet of glass with small, chest-high sets marching toward the shore. Low tide would be later in the day, and as long as the gentle northwest breeze continued, the swells would continue and make for an enjoyable afternoon.

I stretched my legs a little and crossed A1A to return to the marina. There still wasn't much traffic, but an unusual feeling of being watched overcame me as I started down Eau Gallie. I kept my eyes peeled, but saw nothing.

Finally arriving back at the boat, I set the coffeemaker to brew and headed to the shower. To my pleasant surprise, it was occupied.

"Nice jog?" she called out from the shower over the stream of running water.

I didn't answer, but slipped out of my sweatshirt and shorts.

"Tuck, is that you?" came a more concerned voice.

"Who did you expect?" was my reply as I slid into the shower and wrapped my arms around her waist and nibbled on her wet neck.

She smiled. "You never know who might drop by," she said as she arched her back. "The other day it was the old sailor from the other side of the marina who stopped by. I actually was hoping for the little bald guy from Orlando, who shows up on the weekends."

"You mean the little guy with the cute younger wife?" I answered. "That figures, throw me over for a more mature man with mucho dollars."

"Nah, you'll do." She smiled as she turned to face me and wrap her arms around my neck. "We have a few minutes before we have to leave for work." Her eyebrows lifted mischievously.

She slowly placed her lips on mine and worked her tongue around my mouth as she lifted her left leg and wrapped it around my waist. Leaning back and placing her hands on the wall, she rose to meet me and rocked gently underneath the trickling water as the pleasure overcame both of us.

CHAPTER

21

I took the scenic ride to the office that took me up A1A past Satellite Beach, my soon-to-be new hometown. The ride was uneventful as I passed Patrick Air Force Base and entered Cocoa Beach. The CD player blurted out the lyrics to my favorite Skynyrd songs. I rolled down the window to let in the morning breeze, then made a left onto the Minuteman Causeway and headed to the mainland.

I arrived at the office feeling good, especially after my morning shower with Karla. The more I thought about her, the more my mind just said "Wow."

The office buzzed with a breaking story, so I headed to Mitch's office to find out exactly what was going on.

"Morning, Tucker," came the greeting from Martha, Mitch's secretary.

"Good morning, Martha. You're looking lovely today," I said, proceeding to his door. "Is he in?"

"You're so full of it, Tucker," she said with a chuckle. "Yes, he's in and actually waiting for you. Go right in."

I blew Martha a puckered kiss, turned the door knob, and stepped into his office.

"Hey, there's my boy," came the greeting as Mitch stood to greet me. A woman rose from in front of his desk and reached out her hand.

She was an attractive woman, very professional looking in a light tan tailored skirt and jacket, long blond hair, and a pretty smile to match.

"Tucker, this is Ms.Greenwood I shook her hand and she sat back down.

Mitch spoke first. "Have a seat, Tucker, Ms Greenwood...it is Ms.?" he asked, turning to get a positive nod from her. "Ms Greenwood is from the *U.S. Globe*. She drove up from Miami just to interview you. I told her you'd be happy to spend a few minutes with her." He gave me a stare that told me to go along with what the reporter wanted.

I now remembered my phone messages and gave Mitch a similar look in return. I sat down and turned to face Ms. Greenwood.

"Please call me Linda," she started. "Tucker, let me get straight to the point. I would like your story on how you contact let's say the spirits from beyond," she paused, "to help you do your investigative reporting..."

I cut her off and spoke. Not to her, but to Mitch. "You're serious? You want me to do this interview?"

He just sat and smirked, never making eye contact with me.

Linda jumped right back in. "Tucker, you have a story that's a seller, and my readers want to know."

"Mitch, you're serious?" I repeated, ignoring the reporter.

Mitch finally turned to face me. "Tucker, I promised Linda that if she came up here, you'd be happy to spend ten minutes of your very busy schedule to speak with her." Now he gave me another serious stare. "It would be a plus for our newspaper if you did an interview."

I sat and stared back at him with my left eye slightly closed to show my frustration. From the corner of it, I noticed Ms...Linda sitting with a look of optimism on her face.

I really had no option, so I looked at her and reluctantly agreed. "Okay, I'll see you for ten minutes, and only for ten minutes. Agreed?"

She smiled. "Great. Let's say we head to your office and we'll get started."

"Tell you what. You head next door and I'll be there in a minute. I need to speak to Mitch for a second."

She smiled, thanked Mitch, and headed to my office.

"Really, Mitch? Really?"

"I know, Tuck, but it's great publicity for the paper, and you can play the interview any way you want. We need to strike while the iron's hot. C'mon, buddy, do it for the team. I'll make it worth your while."

Here he goes again with the sports analogies. Might as well suck it up and go along with it...again.

"Okay, Mitch. But I'm playing it my way."

"That's my boy." He stood up and slapped my back.

"Oh, by the way, what's all the commotion about this new story today?" I questioned.

"That's my something special for you. The sheriff's department just found a car or something with two bodies inside. It's in a retention pond out past 520. I saved it for you knowing you'd want to check it out. If your buddy Craig is on the case you can get the inside scoop."

"Damn straight I would. I'll head over right away and see what's going on," I said excitedly, heading for the door.

"Hold on there, slick," he replied. "Head out in ten minutes, after you speak to Ms. Greenwood."

I stopped at the door in midstride, gave him the middle finger, and smiled as I walked out the door.

CHAPTER

22

I hopped in my Jeep and headed north on US 1. Turning left on 520 and over the railroad tracks, I set my course west toward the outer region of Brevard County.

With the window down and wind whipping in, I turned on my radio and enjoyed the ride, soon passing under Interstate 95. There was little traffic as I played my hand against the strength of the wind outside my window. I felt a tingle of excitement for my new assignment as I drove.

The ride would take me about fifteen minutes, just enough time to rehash my interview with Linda Greenwood.

The first two questions she had asked me were: Tucker, are the spirits that visit covered in white sheets the way many people visualize them? Are they scary?

I had smiled and kept my composure, all the time wondering if she had any viable synapses between her ears.

"No," I had answered calmly. "The visits I receive are from my Seminole great-uncle. The Seminole Indians are a very spiritual people. They are proud and take their beliefs very seriously. So the connection with my ancestor was, and is, an extraordinary personal event that I take a great deal of pride in."

I knew she wanted to play my entire experience up and dramatize it for her gossip rag, so I just went at her with the truth, holding nothing back. I didn't lose my cool as she probably had hoped, so she just sat staring at me in disbelief.

We sat in silence for a full thirty seconds until she finally replied, "Oh, I didn't realize you took this so seriously."

"Well, you wanted the truth, didn't you? I'm very proud of my heritage."

After a number of other questions, ranging from what I visualized to the passing of my nana, we ended the interview.

"Thank you, Tucker," she said as I left. "I'll work on the piece and e-mail you a copy before we go to print. When I'm done, I think you'll be happy with the story."

So that was that. Whatever she wrote, whatever angle she took, I could care less. It was time for me to step up to the plate and stand up for what I believed in.

As I sped along 520, I passed the junction for 532 and traveled another mile or so. The area was not one I was familiar with, yet a sense of familiarity washed over me. I had the distinct feeling I had been in the area before.

I drove a little farther and finally entered an area marked by a number of sheriff's cars and satellite news vans. I pulled to the right onto the grass and jumped out. Again, though I was positive I had never been here, an eerie sensation of awareness washed over me. I knew this place. From where, I wasn't sure.

Yellow crime scene tape, hung across a dirt path leading into the underbrush, kept the reporters at bay. Many were busy setting up camera angles for their next newscast.

I walked past a group of people and headed toward the first deputy I saw standing guard.

"Can I help you?" the deputy asked as I approached and continued with, "Sorry, sir, but no onlookers beyond this point."

A second officer wandered over and eyed me over his sunglasses. I answered, "Is Detective Craig Williams on the scene?"

"Yes, he is," was the curt response I received.

"Could you please radio him? My name is Tucker Ander—"

"I know who you are, sir," the newly arrived sergeant answered with a grin. "I'll radio him and see if he's available."

Craig arrived within minutes, lifting the crime tape for me to join him. I nodded to the deputies and started to walk down the path.

"Tuck, I thought you'd show up eventually." He started to fill me in. "We have a Chevy pickup, partly submerged, with two bodies inside. The remains are in rough shape. A male and female, Caucasian, and fairly young. Teenagers."

"Who found the pickup?"

Craig halted. "Well, nobody found it. The vehicle was totally submerged. With the dry conditions we've had of late, the pond's water level dropped and the roof of the truck became visible. At that point, seems the On-Star system kicked in and the location was identified by satellite. We got the call this morning, and here we are." Craig rubbed the bridge of his nose and absently ran his hand through his hair.

"Damn. Technology is getting unbelievable," I mumbled as we continued our walk around the bend toward the crime's location.

"It gets better," Craig continued. "As the report reads, the truck occupants are two teens from Texas who were heading to Cocoa Beach. Parents have been looking for them for over a month now."

I chimed in, "A relationship gone bad type of deal? Murder-suicide?"

Craig shook his head no. "The boy took Daddy's ride, skipped town with his little girlfriend, and somewhere along the line they end up in the wrong place at the worst time."

"What makes you say that?" I asked.

Craig lifted his sunglasses and stared at me. "Tuck, their hands were zip-tied behind their backs and their throats were cut…almost to the point of decapitation. We've got a real problem here."

"Maybe a drug deal gone bad," I suggested.

"Nah, don't think so. The kids don't need to come all the way to Florida for that. They can get whatever they want along the Mexican border back home."

Craig and I continued to walk. About one hundred yards farther, we came to the mud-encrusted vehicle. Crews were working to gather evidence as the silver pickup sat to the side, still dripping water from the bed.

Craig spoke. "This is scary shit, Tuck. I've been doing this for a long time, and I don't have a good feeling about any of this."

"I know," I said. "You never get used to it."

"What really bothers me, Tuck, is they're only kids, and the manner in which they were murdered. Or should I say executed."

Craig's last word, *executed*, sent a shiver down my spine.

"It's scary. We both have teens, Tuck. And something like this… well…it's just scary as hell."

I didn't know what to say. I just stood and patted Craig on the back.

"I guess Karla will be doing the autopsy on this one," I said, shading my eyes from the afternoon glare.

"Yeah," Craig answered. "Hope you two didn't have anything planned tonight. This is going to keep her busy for a while."

"Detective?" came a voice over the radio.

"Yes," he answered.

"Sir, I think you better get out here. We're having a small a problem at the entrance," retorted the agitated voice.

CHAPTER

23

Craig and I walked briskly back toward the main road. As we rounded the corner, a large black Lincoln Navigator blocked our path.

Two men in suits and wearing sunglasses exited the vehicle as we approached.

"Detective Williams? My name is John Dentino. I'm with the attorney general's office." He flashed his ID to Craig who glanced at it. "This is Special Agent Ferguson. We'll be relieving you and your team of this investigation."

"You're what?" exclaimed Craig with a vigor I hadn't seen in years. "This is under the jurisdiction of the Brevard County Sheriff's Office!"

"Detective, we don't have time to mince words with you. Your commander will update you as soon as you call him back at your office," the special agent said.

Craig pulled his cell from his holster and walked over to the tree line to talk in private.

As I stood with the agents, for some reason I was drawn to the big Lincoln. The windows were tinted, but with the angle from the sun, I was able to make out the silhouettes of two figures sitting in the rear. Their identities were hidden, but the feeling that a set of evil eyes watched me could not be denied.

I started to walk toward the vehicle when I was abruptly stopped by the other agent.

"And you're going where?" he asked as he gripped my shoulder.

Now being touched, especially by someone I don't know, and an individual with an attitude, is something I don't take pleasure in.

I froze, stared at his hand on my arm before saying, "Excuse me?"

I slowly removed his hand, ignored him, and continued walking toward the SUV. "I was just wondering if I could bother someone for a cigarette and a light."

I could now see the shadowy figures moving about as I came a little closer. Ten feet away, the other agent finally spoke up. "Stop and move away from the vehicle."

I turned and looked at the two men now standing at my side.

"Is there a problem, Agent, or is someone in there that doesn't want to be seen?"

Neither man answered.

"Let's go, Tucker," was the next voice I heard coming from Craig as he approached. "It's all theirs. Let's get the fuck out of here."

Both men smiled as Craig took my arm and escorted me away.

"There is a time and place for everything, and now's not the time or place."

Looking back over my shoulder, I could sense a strange set of eyes following me as we made our exit.

"Tucker, this thing smells rotten to the core. Something is happening here that isn't good. And we need to get to the bottom of it."

CHAPTER

24

Colonel Trout sat rubbing the sides of his throbbing head with his thumbs, cradling his forehead against his pointer fingers. The berating he had just received over the phone, as well as his lack of knowledge about certain events, was more than enough to prompt his headache and embarrass the shit out of him.

He had called for his men to return immediately to the command center, and now he sat in deep thought about how to deal with his two renegade operatives.

The hum of two quads gradually increased as they approached the trailer and slowly came to a stop. Sounds of muffled footsteps led up the metal stairs and into the center.

"Sir!" Jesus and Jack snapped to attention, arms at their sides in front of the colonel. "Reporting as ordered, sir."

"At ease," retorted Trout as he lifted his head to face the two men in front of him. "Take a seat, gentlemen."

Jack and Jesus glanced at each other. The order to sit was an unusual invitation coming from the colonel.

A strange silence hung in the air as the men sat. The colonel stood to look out the window over the barren landscape that he had learned to loathe.

"I've asked you to come in 'cause there seems to have been an incident that I wasn't made aware of."

Both men looked at the back of the colonel's head, nodded, and then looked at each other.

Trout continued, "Now, have you two done anything in the last month or so that you...let's say...forgot to report? Maybe something like the old squatter's murder a while back?"

The men just sat silently.

"Very well then, let me fill you in. There has just been a pickup truck recovered from a retention pond about four miles from here. Now, mind you, the truck was not in our sector, but the proximity of the location has brought unwanted scrutiny to the area. Is that understood?"

` Both men answered by nodding their heads. Trout turned from the window and glared at his two subordinates with his hands clasped behind his back. Using his height, he strategically placed himself alongside the two men, giving him a psychological advantage as he looked down on them.

He continued, "Now, gentlemen, let me make this perfectly clear to you one last time. In no way, shape, or form are you to act independently of this office. If you do decide to take matters into your own hands again, the matter will be taken from me and handled by people higher up that you will not want to deal with. Is that understood?"

"Yes, sir," quickly replied both men.

"And anything you see as a clear and present danger to this mission will not be acted upon until you get clearance from me. I have twenty other agents in the field, and you two are assigned to the most sensitive location. You need to be on top of your game here. Got it?"

Both men again answered yes.

The colonel paused before going on. "In no way are you to engage any perpetrators with extreme prejudice. You are now in a reconnaissance status. Just report to me, it's that simple. Is that perfectly clear?"

"Clear as day, sir."

"Good. We only have a few weeks left in this godforsaken hell hole, so don't fuck it up. Now you two get the hell out of here and see if you can complete the mission without causing any further damage."

The two men rose to their feet, saluted while avoiding eye contact with the colonel, and exited out the back of the trailer.

Colonel Trout's gaze followed the two men as they walked toward their vehicles.

Damn, if I were in South America again I wouldn't give two shits what they did…but here it's a different ballgame, and it's going to make me rich.

* * *

Jesus looked at Jack as they mounted their quads. "I told you doing those two kids was a bad idea."

"Oh, stop your whining," replied Jack. "We disposed of the remains at a different site. Just blind luck they found it."

"Yeah, but they did," was Jesus's reply. "We can't be messing up like that anymore."

Jack glared before saying, "Asshole, you weren't complaining when we worked that little sweet thing over and you had your way with her while the boyfriend watched, now did ya?"

Jesus shrugged his shoulders as they fired up their engines and headed out to the old squatter's shack they now made their own.

CHAPTER

25

My mind ran wild with speculation about the newly discovered crime. The location, how the sheriff's department was taken off the investigation, the occupants of the Lincoln Navigator all led to a feeling of uneasiness that now crept over me.

The day was still young and I had a few hours to kill before I picked up Carl for our surf session and performed my final walk-through on the condo. It actually was my midweek visitation day with the kids. Jessie kept herself involved in school activities, but Carl had finally shown interest in surfing, which made it easier for us to interact. To be honest, I had been having trouble finding ways to occupy his attention since I was not a cartoon or video game, so surfing turned out to be the perfect outlet that we could both relate to.

Making it back to the paper with little traffic on US 1 to slow me down, I went directly to my office, dodging the usual questions of curiosity from the staff: Who was it? Where were they from? How were they murdered? Those were just a few of the questions I couldn't give a straight answer to.

I was logging onto my computer when Mitch popped in.

"So, partner, what'd we find out?" was the first question he asked as he sat down across from me.

I swiveled in my chair and gazed at Mitch, deep in thought.

"I really can't say. It's all a little strange."

Mitch crossed his legs. "You can't say or you won't say? You must have an idea. Wasn't your buddy Craig on the scene?"

I nodded my head yes and went on. "It just doesn't add up, Mitch. The victims were two kids from Texas. They were found in a submerged pickup. No one would have ever found it if it weren't for the dry weather we've been having and the water level in the pond dropping three feet."

Mitch continued to listen in silence, drumming his fingers on the edge of my desk. "Okay, this thing really is a bit unusual, but Tuck, it's not like we haven't had a murder before. Why do you think this one is so strange?"

"You're right, Mitch, we've had murders, but our sheriff's office has never been taken off the case before. They were removed by the attorney general's office. I was standing right there when they showed up; they caught everyone by surprise and immediately took over without any explanation or even questioning what was known so far. These were just two kids. The girl was my daughter's age."

Mitch's eyes widened.

I continued, "The sheriff's office's CSI unit is one of the best in the state, Mitch. So why remove them from this case, especially when the kids were obviously executed?"

"Executed?" Mitch exploded in surprise.

"Yes, executed, Mitch. Hands tied behind their backs with zip-ties and their necks sliced, almost to the point of decapitation."

"Maybe it was gang or drug related?"

"No, I don't think so. A gang or a pissed-off dealer would want the bodies in plain sight, to send a clear message to others. Plus they would have shot their victims, not used a knife. Whoever did this clearly wanted the bodies gone forever. It's rare to find a throat slashing and hard as hell to cut someone's throat so deep."

You could tell by his expression that Mitch was getting his game face on as he asked with curiosity, "Is Karla still going to be working on the case?"

"I would think so, unless they decide to transport the remains all the way out to Orange County. She's planning on meeting me later for my condo walk-through, so I'll call her in a bit and see what's up."

Mitch got up to leave and tapped my desk with his knuckles three times. "Okay, this is all yours, buddy, stay on top of it, and keep me in the loop. Remember, we're a team, okay, Captain?"

I always get a kick out of Mitch when he uses sports analogies with me as he's the most un-jock person I know. But I go along with it, why hurt his feelings, he's a pretty cool guy.

"You got it, teammate." I smiled while giving him a thumbs-up.

Grabbing his attention once more before he left, I yelled out, "Hey, Mitch, whatever I find, we're going with it all the way, okay?"

Mitch smiled and winked before closing the door behind him.

I turned to face my computer and immediately jumped to the Google search engine, typing in a few ideas, when I noticed my in-box icon flashing. "What the…"

I hit the mail icon and saw the usual trash before noticing one that stood out. "Read Me – Important." I clicked the message. It read:

It's all about Coastal Access. All of your questions will be answered.

I tried to reveal the sender, but it was not shown, and I had no success with trying to retrace the URL.

"Coastal Access?" I said aloud. What the hell could that be all about?

CHAPTER 26

Leaving the office on my way to pick up Carl, I was again overwhelmed by an uneasy feeling in the pit of my stomach. My dreams, the recently discovered murders, the peculiar e-mail I had received about coastal access all made me wonder what could happen next. Then there was the area of the crime that had somehow given me a feeling of déjà vu.

While sitting at the traffic light, I picked up my cell and punched in Karla's number.

"Hi, honey," came the welcome greeting I received when she answered.

I placed her on speaker phone as the traffic started to move.

"Honey'? You always answer the phone that way?" I asked with a laugh.

"Funny, knucklehead. You do know I have caller ID."

"Yeah, yeah, sure. I bet you say that to all your callers. Listen, sweetie, are you going to be able to make it to the walk-through?"

She sounded disappointed. "I was going to call you, but I'm sure you already know about the two kids they found on the other side of Interstate 95."

"Yeah, real shitty. I was just out there with Craig."

"Well, I'll give you three guesses who has the autopsy assignment for them."

"Let me guess…ummm, you?" I acted surprised, but they'd be stupid to choose anyone else; she was one of the best in her field.

"Of course me, you nut job. But I guess you kinda figured that out anyway. I'm so sorry I can't make your walk-through today."

"Oh, I can handle it. I'll have Carl with me as my sidekick." I wouldn't pick him up till after the walk-through, but it sounded good and eased her mind.

"Great, then I hope the two of you have fun together today. And please be careful when you go surfing; you're not fifteen years old anymore."

"Careful? Who me? You're talking to the original Beach Boy."

A giggle came from the other end.

I continued, "I will. I'm really excited to see what Carl can do. I bet he'll be a chip off the old block."

"Hold on a minute." Karla's voice disappeared from the phone and returned a few seconds later. "Gotta go, Tuck. The bodies just arrived. I'll call you later if I find anything. Better get to work. Love you," she said quickly before the phone went dead.

"Find anything?" It would be interesting if she did. As Craig had said, this looked like a professional job. If anyone could find a clue, it would be Karla.

CHAPTER

27

I met my real estate agent, Kathy Hile, at the condo to receive the keys. She had found the perfect place for me a month ago and had handled all the necessary paperwork. After a quick look around, I signed the last document and became a new homeowner. Without any furniture to sit on until tomorrow, I decided to head over a little early and pick up Carl.

Honeymoon Lake resonated with affluence. Homes were meticulously kept and driveways were littered with luxury cars. My children's home was no different.

As I pulled down the driveway toward my ex-wife's house, I saw that Carl was already outside waiting for me.

"Hi, Dad. What took you so long?" he beamed as he ran up to greet me with his surfboard under his arm.

I left the Jeep to help him place his board on the roof rack, but he had already scrambled up the hood and was in the process of strapping it down next to my board.

"Hi, partner. What do you mean late? I'm not supposed to be here for another thirty minutes. You ready to hit the surf?" I said as I reached out to grab his hips and lift him back down to the ground.

"Yeah, Dad. I know you're early. I was so excited I couldn't sleep. I've been waiting since dawn. Let's go!"

I smiled. It was then that I noticed the board on the roof was not his usual ride.

"Where's the old twin fin I gave you?"

"Oh, that old thing? It's in the garage, Dad. You're going to like my new board. Mom and Charles brought me to the surf shop last weekend to pick it up."

"Really?" I was stunned. "Your mother actually decided to support your surfing interest and spend some money on a board?"

Carl choked a little on his words as he spoke. "Ah, not really. Charlie was the one who actually bought it for me. Mom really didn't say much about it. Charlie's a really cool guy, Dad, and easy to talk to."

"Really? He's easy to talk to?"

"You know, Dad. He's not you," he said with a smile, "but sometimes I'd rather deal with him when I get in trouble. Mom can be so strict."

"Well, Carl. Your mom is strict because she cares. So go easy on her. If Charles can be the mediator between you two, great. But don't be so hard on her."

Wonderful, just what every dad wants to hear. His son's stepdad was a great guy and maybe easier to talk to than me. I'll admit, even though it wasn't something I wanted to hear from Carl, I was glad the guy was treating my kids well.

"He actually took me to the beach before school a couple of times this week so I could get a session in."

"Really?" I repeated, trying not to sound too jealous. *Son of a bitch, this guy is trying to steal my kid away from me; it's obvious surfing is the only thing Carl and I enjoy together, so why not move in? Damn.*

We headed over the Pineda Causeway and hit the first parking lot in front of Patrick Air Force Base. We talked about the usual surf things, from his idol, Kelly Slater, to the coming events in the area. We took down the boards and headed over the dune walk with our wet suits. We were greeted by a glassy ocean, a breeze out of the northwest, and two- to three-foot sets; perfect for a nine-year-old and his aging father.

I watched in delight as my boy waxed his own board and pulled on his wet suit. The sight made me wonder if I had looked like Carl when I first began surfing a long time ago.

"That's one sharp board you got there; how'd Charles know which board to get you?"

"Isn't it hot, Dad?" Carl went on excitedly, "He special ordered it through Quiet Flight. It's got hard smooth rails, quad fins that grip the face like no other, and a deep single concave to a double vee off the tail. It's really fast and responsive. It's so gnarly. I love it!"

Jealously reared its ugly head, and I was really having a hard time hiding it. No point in denying the truth.

We ran into the surf and glided our boards over the wash, then started to paddle until we made it to the lineup. Not many people around, which was nice for a day as perfect as this.

"Now Carl, remember to dig your tail into the wave and—"

"I know, Dad. Mom and Charlie got lessons for me over in Cocoa Beach."

What the fuck. New board and lessons. I'm not liking where this is headed. But hey, I'll try to remain calm and enjoy the day.

"Okay, kid. Lessons or not, watch and learn from your old man. It's been a while, but it's like riding a bike. I was a slasher back in the day. So get ready to take some notes."

I saw an approaching set on the horizon and paddled to my left to get in position. I spun around, dropped my weight on my tail, and took two strokes, feeling myself being lifted. Jumping to my feet was not a problem, and as the wave started to peel to my right, I set a line down the small face, pushing my weight to the inside. I was doing great until I caught my inside rail and did a face plant into the crest of the wave, tumbling over the falls. I flipped over and got caught in the wash, rolling a few times before resurfacing. My nose was full of water as I came up coughing and shaking my head.

"You really want me to do it like that, Dad?" came the wise-ass remark from my son.

Carl laughed and turned his board to the shoreline as a new set came through. He dug his tail into the wave, took two strokes, and was up in a second dropping down the face and carving hard off the bottom. A quick turn sent him back up the face where he proceeded to snap his board off the top and return to his aggressive dismantling of the wave's face as he disappeared down the line.

Popping up over the soup at the end of the ride, he dropped down onto his board and proceeded to paddle back in my direction.

"Wow. Carl, that was awesome," was all I could say.

"Thanks, Dad," he replied as he glided up to me and sat upright on his board. "I really got a lot better with the lessons Charles bought for me." With that, he must have seen the hurt look on my face and added, "But you know, it's really in my genes."

I smiled and relaxed, and the rest of the two hours went by in a flash.

"It's getting late, Carl. I've got to get you home before your mom gets piss…mad at me again."

"I know, Dad, just one more ride," he commanded as he took off down the line toward the beach and the slowly setting sun.

I sat alone in the water for a minute and felt content. I was proud of my son, and regardless of the new board or purchased lessons, it felt good to see him becoming accomplished in a sport he loved.

The red sun flickered behind a large, puffy cloud on the western horizon when I noticed a woman standing and watching us from the beach. She was a vibrant-looking elderly lady and stood with arms folded and a smile across her face. I shaded my eyes from the reappearing sun. Shadows cast by the clouds played tricks with my eyes. Dark and light stretched in various shades across the sand. I looked and finally located the woman as she stood at the water's edge. It was then that I realized who she was, and with the blink of an eye, the vision of my nana was gone.

CHAPTER

28

The ride home with Carl was a quiet one. We grabbed a bite to eat at Long Dogger's and finally reached Honeymoon Lake as the sunny day faded into dark. Carl yawned. Exhausted from the day's activity, I helped him unload his board and carry his gear toward the garage.

All of a sudden a Beamer roared into the driveway behind us and honked its horn. No one emerged from the car, but my daughter came running out of the house and breezed past us.

"Hi, Daddy, bye, Daddy, gotta run!" my daughter said as she whizzed past me.

"Whoa there, hold on, honey!" I shouted as Jessie finally came to a halt just prior to reaching the car. She retraced her steps and backed up to me in obvious disgust, but I still forced out a smile and a kiss on the cheek from her.

"Sorry, Daddy."

"Jessie, where you heading off to in such a hurry?"

"Oh, Wayne and I are headed over to Cocoa; a friend of his is having a party."

The car horn blasted twice more, and my agitated daughter's eyes darted between her waiting boyfriend and me.

Although I was getting pissed, I tried to stay calm as I redirected her attention. "Well, listen, Jessie," I grabbed her hands to hold her concentration as I darted evil daggers toward the impatient Beamer, "You be careful. If you have any problems at all, you have my cell number."

"God, Dad, I am just going to a party, not college," she said as she pulled her hands away.

I smiled for a second because she was still interested in college, but then I got serious. "And Jessie—" She turned to look at me once more before grabbing the handle of the door. "Remember, you're to be treated like a princess, don't except anything less!" That comment was intended for the jerk in the car.

She smiled at me as she pulled the door open and blew me a kiss. Hopefully she smiled because she remembered "princess" was the nickname I gave her when she was a toddler.

I watched the car pull away with a squeal of tires. I had an over-whelming feeling of dislike for this Wayne character.

"I don't trust that little fuck," I caught myself mumbling aloud as Carl stood next to me and chimed in.

"I ditto that one, Dad."

I looked down at him and we both laughed aloud.

I rubbed his head as he responded, "Really, Dad, there is some-thing about that dude that's really weird."

"Weird? How so?"

"Just weird, Dad. Kinda a guy I don't trust," Carl answered.

"Wow, Carl, you really feel that way?"

"Yeah, Dad, what Jess does is her own business, at least that's what she tells me every day, but that guy's a real slimer. He's got Mom all fooled just because his dad is some hot shot nervous surgeon."

"That's a neurosurgeon," I added with a chuckle.

"Yeah, whatever. He's still a dirt bag." Carl shrugged his shoulders.

I couldn't help but grin. Carl truly was a chip off the old block.

"Thanks for taking me out today, Dad. It was awesome," he said as he hugged my waist.

I gave my son, now becoming a young man, a huge hug and told him as soon as I settled into the condo we could do some serious surfing since the condo was across the street from an awesome break.

With a smile, we parted. I steered my Jeep onto Tropical Trail, the quickest route to my last night's stay at Mitch's yacht.

* * *

Dusk had completely settled in and I noticed the light on my cell phone flashing as I continued south. Taking a minute, I pulled over and saw there were actually two messages. The first was from Karla telling me she would be longer than expected. The second was from Craig.

"Hey, buddy," came the familiar voice of my childhood friend. "Listen, I checked that kid out for you, you know, the Beamer kid Jessie's dating. The info on him is not what you may want to hear. First of all he's seventeen years old. Seems the bastard has a number of speeding tickets and a few arrests for drugs; weed, to be exact. Apparently Daddy is a big wheeler and dealer with the new hospital, so a lot of his encounters with the law have been expunged. This is all off the record from our department's other folders, if you get my drift."

I did get his drift, knowing that regardless of what the politically correct wanted done, the law enforcement agencies kept their own files. Off the record was sadly true, because no other officer would even admit to these files, let alone share outside the brotherhood.

So the kid was pretty much an entitled asshole. That much I figured from our first encounter. At least my intuition was still intact and in working order. The concern was the kid had my daughter fooled. That was something I'd eventually have to deal with.

The message from Craig continued. "Now for the interesting stuff."

There was more? Where was he going with this? Having my daughter dating a douchey pot head was bad enough, what was worse?

"Tucker, I ran a check on your neighbor Doug." He paused, almost for effect. "Seems he doesn't exist."

I stared at the phone in disbelief as the message continued. "There is no record of birth, marriage, divorce, or even death, for that matter. Sorry, but your new friend is a shadow. I worked it all day and used every resource available to the department, and there simply is no record of his existence. I know your wheels are turning, it's really strange, call me back when you get this message and we'll talk in depth."

With that, the message was over. What did this all mean? Craig had probably screwed something up. That thought only lasted a second. Craig was a little goofy at times, but not about his job. I could honestly say he was one of the best and took his work totally serious.

The strangeness of the events unfolding around me was unnerving, to say the least. But now a neighbor, no, a friend that I felt comfortable sharing things with, might not be the man he says he is? This was unsettling almost to the point of feeling a lump form in my throat. I started the Jeep back up as I strained to wrap my head around things and kept coming back to the question: who the hell is Doug?

CHAPTER

29

The evening was clear and a little warm for this time of year as Jesus and Jack made their rounds along the perimeter of Area 176. Both men were diligent in their duties and had no desire to have the mission compromised so near its completion. The only concern was the weekend campfire parties set up by the local teenagers. There really hadn't been much of a problem containing them in the beginning, but now the kids seemed to sneak a little deeper into the woods to avoid detection from the roadway. They knew this would eventually create an unwanted problem for the operatives from WWSC.

"Hey, Jesus, we better head over and set up our nightly surveillance in the northern sector. Those kids will probably be back out here tonight..."

Jesus just stared through the binoculars held tightly to his face as he quickly shot up a hand to quiet Jack.

"What the hell?" Jack shouted. Don't you hold up your hand to quiet me."

Jesus didn't acknowledge Jack's mini tirade. The look on his face gave Jack a reason to worry for a moment.

Jesus finally spoke. "I swear I just saw something, damn it. Now I can't locate it."

"What the hell are you talking about?"

"I saw something at three o'clock." He pointed to the position with his right hand. "About three clicks low in the marsh. Do you see it?"

Jack dismounted from his quad, walked over to him, and angrily grabbed the binoculars out of Jesus's hands. Placing them to his face, he spoke. "Nothing, I don't see fucking anything, I told you you're getting too much goddamn sun. Now you're seeing things."

"I'm telling you, I saw…well, I saw the same thing as the other day."

"Really," Jack replied sarcastically. "You saw an Indian again?"

Jesus sounded sincere. "I'm serious, Jack, no shitting you." He jerked the binoculars out of Jack's hands and continued to search the woods.

Jack laughed aloud as Jesus looked at him and asked, "What the hell is so funny?"

"I remember now, you keep falling asleep reading that shitty little newspaper. They keep running that article about the county's anniversary celebration."

"Yeah, so what? The paper bores me, so reading always helps put me to sleep," Jesus spat back, not liking being the source of amusement for his partner.

"Don't you remember, they're making this big deal about the Indians that settled this area and some crap about Ponce de Leon."

"Ponce who?" asked Jesus, not liking that Jack was trying to make him feel stupid.

"Never mind, you moron, point is, they keep talking about Indians, so you're probably thinking about them and now you imagine you see one."

Jesus responded, still not laughing, "I think a lot about naked women, but I haven't seen any of them appear out here yet."

Jesus was not one of Jack's favorite people, but he had worked with him long enough in a number of hostile environments to know the man was not pulling his leg.

"He was in a canoe, paddling through the canal straight toward me. I swear I saw him again tonight, and the Indian was looking right at me."

Jack let the silence settle for a minute, then answered, "Tell ya what you need. You need a nice long vacation and a good lay. Come on, let's get moving."

Jack wasn't one for giving in to an argument, but he couldn't lose Jesus now, not when they were so close to receiving the biggest payday of their lives.

Jack slapped Jesus' back. "You crack me up sometimes."

Jesus took one last look before pulling down the binoculars and agreeing. "Yeah, I guess you're right. Must be the hours we're putting in in this godforsaken country."

Both men mounted their quads and slipped off into the distance. The apparition of a lone Indian drifted across the marshland, his eyes trailing the intruders as they made their way on those strange contraptions.

Osci was stern in his diligence. This was his land, the land of his people. To have it exploited by the white devils was not what his ancestors of the great Seminole people had wished for. The apparition began to fade into its surroundings as a lone alligator emerged from its shelter and took the Indian's position.

CHAPTER

30

I arrived back at the marina with little trouble. Traffic along South Tropical Trail was light to nonexistent, with only a few cars and walkers passed along the way. The new knowledge I had about Doug not being who he said he was had sent my senses into overdrive. I was beginning to doubt everything. I beamed my headlights into the few vehicles, becoming suspicious of the occupants. Damn, the mind can be your own worst enemy.

When I arrived, the marina was quiet and the security lights were on. The warm breeze of late afternoon ruffled the palms and gently rocked the boats on their moorings.

I only had a few personal items left to pack, and then I was off to the new condo for hopefully a good night's rest. Most of the furniture I had ordered would be delivered in a few days, but I had no problem roughing it in a place I could now call my own. I had my mattress and priceless art collection of Damien Shared paintings. So in my mind I had the necessities.

I occasionally thought about the belongings I lost in my home fire—okay, trailer explosion—last year. Family photos were the only treasures I missed. I had come to realize that material possessions can always be replaced, so my mind was at ease knowing I would soon make my new place feel like a home.

Approaching my dock, I slowed so I could see if there was any activity on Doug's—or whoever he claimed to be—boat. I noticed a small light on inside, but there didn't appear to be any movements or sounds.

"Hello, Tucker," came the voice from another neighbor who was usually here only on weekends.

"Good evening, John, I'm surprised to see you down here so early in the week," I responded in greeting.

"Oh, had a few comp days to burn up. I figured better use them before I lose them. Besides, I brought my secretary with me for a little dick-tation, if you know what I mean? Plus I'd rather be here than there.

His secretary? Wonder if wife number three knows this. And people call me a perv?

"It's pretty quiet around here tonight, glad to see another body."

"Yeah," I answered. "Actually kinda nice. Doug and I are the only regulars in this section. Oh, by the way, have you seen him tonight?"

I figured I'd take the opportunity to see if someone else's eyes saw anything different than what mine may have missed.

"Doug? Well, yeah, funny you should ask. I passed him when I first pulled in. He actually was coming off your boat. I said hi and just moved on. Thought you were in there too."

I gave him a quizzical look that caught him by surprise, and he continued, "I hope it's okay, Doug being in your place and all. God, I am not such a good neighbor, I didn't even think to ask anything about it. Seeing how you two seem so tight and all."

"No, no, John, it's no problem," I lied to reassure him. "He was probably putting back the charts he borrowed the other day."

"Yeah, that's probably it," he lied too, obviously feeling guilty for not questioning him. "I'll let you get on with your packing. Enjoy your move to the condo," John said, walking away.

Now I know I'm probably a little jumpy, but what the hell did John say he was here for? Comp days? A little R&R with his secretary? An eerie felling made the hairs on the back of my neck stand on end. I didn't recall ever saying I was packing and moving to a new condo. How did he know that?

I quickly turned to watch John as he reached the end of the walkway, where he turned the corner and peered back at me before he finally disappeared.

SHIT, am I imagining things?

I continued the rest of the way down the dock and cautiously stepped aboard. Everything appeared, on the surface, to be in the order I left it. Although who really pays careful attention to their surroundings, especially in their own home?

My eyes took a few seconds to adjust to the light as I stepped down into the boat's massive saloon. My senses were now tuned to every noise the boat uttered.

I jumped as the cell phone in my pocket startled me, but quickly exhaled as I recognized the familiar chime. I was happy to hear Karla's voice on the other end.

"Hi, kitten, nice to hear the sound of your voice," was my greeting as I continued to slowly look around the room.

"Hey, baby, I'm running a little late with these two bodies, so I'll crash at my place tonight and see you tomorrow."

"Oh, okay," I answered with a disheartened sigh.

She heard the tone of my voice and added, "Don't worry, we'll christen the condo tomorrow night. I'm sure you can hold out a day." She giggled.

"Yeah, yeah, promises, promises, maybe I'll christen the place myself."

She laughed aloud. "You're disgusting. One more day's not going to kill ya. Plus getting a good night's sleep away from a bear of a snorer like you will be a plus."

"Hold on there, you're the one who snores, not me," I countered, trying to lighten the disappointed of not being together.

"Oh well, I have to get back to work. I'll let you get back to whatever perverted thing you're doing or planning on doing. By the way, what are you doing?"

"Not much. I just got back and wanted to finish packing a few more things before heading over to Satellite, then I have…"

It was then I saw a note, folded up on the navigation station. It read:

Tucker,

We need to sit down and talk. I have some very important information that I need to share with you. I have to run a few errands downtown in Melbourne. I'll catch you later or see you tomorrow.

~Doug

"Hello, hello, you there, Tuck?" Karla was yelling into the phone.

"Ah yeah, honey, right here, sorry, I was just reading a note I found from Doug. I gotta go, we'll talk later, bye."

Karla started to respond, "Okay, baby, love you—" but before she could continue I hung up the phone.

I cut her off unconsciously as I continued to stare at the note, as if some more information would sudden appear on it.

What the hell could this all mean? What information?

CHAPTER

31

Old downtown Melbourne is one of those quaint old southern towns that retained its charm from days gone by. Boutiques, mom and pop shops, restaurants, and a bar or two lined the pristine neighborhood nestled on the bank of the Indian River.

From a side street an older gentleman who went by the alias of Doug made his way along the tree-lined sidewalk, illuminated by the neon lights reflecting from the various businesses.

He had just left the law firm that had represented his family for years. The sole surviving partner was surprised by the unexpected visit, but nevertheless took delivery of the documents needed to update Doug's file.

What Doug didn't notice upon leaving the office were the two younger men who emerged from a sidewalk eatery, intent on monitoring his every movement, as they had since Doug was first spotted in the Brevard area.

One of the men spoke quietly into his cell phone as they followed at a safe distance. "Got him in our sights."

The taller of the two continued, "He's heading west on East New Haven Avenue, crossing the railroad tracks. We'll stay on him till we reach the municipal parking lot."

"Ten-four, sir, we'll pick him up at the lot. You two hustle over to the marina and await further instructions."

Doug continued his walk until he reached the 1987 Mustang he had purchased when he first arrived back in Florida.

"Excuse me, I believe it's Doug, the name you're going by?" were the words from a large, burly man as he approached Doug.

Doug started to backpedal. As he turned away, he came face to face with a second man, just as large as the first.

"Will you be kind enough to accompany us?" the first thug asked.

"Nah, I think I'll pass on that invite, but thanks anyway," Doug responded.

Smiling, the second man answered him, "You don't have a choice, my man, better for you not to resist. My boss hasn't seen you in a long, long time and would like to catch up."

With that, Doug left his vehicle and disappeared into the waiting Town Car. The sedan slowly exited the lot and proceeded to disappear into the flow of traffic.

CHAPTER

32

Wayne took the usual route to the remote western part of Brevard County, the path all the kids took when headed to the woods
parties. Jessie Anderson sat beside him, playing with the audio system, thrilled to be considered a cool kid who was lucky enough to
be invited to a gathering with upperclassmen.

Though alcohol and pot were always in abundance, she had the
self-control to say no when asked to participate. She just chilled
with her new friends, enjoyed the music, and watched the antics
of the other teens.

A big red ball sank on the horizon as dusk settled in. For the
first time Jessie looked up at the road they were now traveling.

"Wayne, this isn't where we usually go. Didn't we just pass the
entrance?" The little Beamer bounced as she noticed Wayne slow-
ing down, looking for the dirt road off Route 532.

"You're right, Jess. We did pass the old entrance. We're going to this awesome new place that Alan found the other night. It's really cool and not too far from the fire pit we usually chill at. It's just a shack out in the middle of nowhere. We'll have it all to ourselves. Besides, the other spot was getting way too crowded with all the geeks from school."

Jessie started to feel a little uneasy as concern crept up inside her. After another two miles, with just enough sunlight to show the opening in the trees, Wayne slowed down and entered the new entrance.

"Wayne, be careful. You'll bottom out and ruin the suspension," she exclaimed as the car dropped off the macadam and pushed past an open gate.

"Don't sweat it. Mom will make Pops buy me a new car if anything happens to this. I'll just bitch and complain and get my way as usual," Wayne countered with a devilish grin. "And why are you so concerned? I don't give a shit about some lousy suspension."

Jessie just looked out the window without response and thought to herself, *He's such a spoiled brat, but he is one of the most popular kids around and such a cutie.*

The dirt road evened out as the trees created a canopy of dense foliage enveloping the tiny vehicle. The sun had now fully set and complete darkness shrouded the teens as they continued to drive deeper into the woods.

Jessie looked around. "I don't like the looks of this, Wayne."

He peered ahead as he flashed on his high beams. "Oh, only a little further. It's cool, sweet thing. Alan and Debbie are already there getting the party started. We're going to have an awesome time tonight, just you wait and see."

As the Beamer finally came to a stop, Jessie saw a rundown shack with Alan's red SUV parked beside it. A pale yellow light reflected through the small windows, just bright enough to show the shack even existed in the underbrush.

"Wayne, I thought you said this was going to be a party? Where is everybody?"

"It is a party, mine and yours. Let's go in and get comfortable."

Wayne jumped out of the vehicle, leaving Jessie sitting alone in the car. Her intuition told her not to follow, but she slowly opened the car door, hesitated, and finally entered the cabin.

In the small structure, Jessie heard moans coming from a sleeping bag lying in the corner. Debbie sat astride Alan, rocking gently back and forth meeting his thrusts from below. Stretching her arms above her head, Debbie glanced toward the newly arrived couple and smiled, not breaking the rhythmic stride or losing concentration from the obvious pleasure she was receiving from below.

"Hey, dude," Wayne interjected as Alan pulled his face away from sucking Debbie's nipples.

"Hey, my man," Alan answered, now lying fully on his back, cupping Debbie's supple breasts. She moaned louder and rocked harder, rubbing the secret spot below her pelvis with trembling fingers. Alan continued, "About time you two got here. Sorry, we couldn't wait. We had to start without you. You know how Deb gets when she's horny. Why don't you two grab a brew and take a hit of the joint I have over there?"

Jessie stood in shock at the scene unfolding in front of her.

Wayne went over and inhaled the remains of the joint first, then popped open a beer while watching Debbie sway on top of his best friend.

"Come on, sweet thing," Wayne said as he grabbed Jessie by the arm and pulled her toward him. "This is our night to party."

"Wayne, are you serious? You think I came all the way out here to have sex with you?" she whispered.

Debbie's moaning increased as she continued to grind her hips, faster and faster until her body shuddered to a climax.

"Oh, you know you want it. You've wanted a piece of the Wayneman ever since you first saw me."

He pulled Jessie closer, wrapping his free arm around her waist while grabbing her breast and biting her neck. She struggled to pull away, seeing the other couple now smiling at them. Her arms were pinned by Wayne's hug as he smashed his groin into her repeatedly.

"You're out of your fucking mind," she stammered, spinning around and forcing herself from his grip. "First of all, who said I wanted to have sex with you? And if I did, it wouldn't be in this shit hole."

Anger now started to show on Wayne's face as he let her go, reaching for another beer and puffing on the pot.

"Fucking A. You knew exactly what I wanted the moment you jumped into my sweet ride. And now I'm going to give it to ya."

Alan and Debbie now stood in various states of undress, watching intently as they started to put on their clothes.

"Take me home, Wayne, now!" Jessie demanded as she turned to face the pot-smoking teen.

He ignored her as the other couple came over to take a hit of the joint. He once again grabbed Jessie, and this time he forced his mouth on hers. Jessie tried to push him away before biting his lip.

"Ouch, you bitch!" Wayne screamed, violently pushing Jessie to the floor as blood trickled from the corner of his mouth. "You have no idea who you're fucking with."

Tension grew as the couple backed away and Alan spoke. "Hey, bud, chill. Let's blow this scene. We can come back another time.

Let's head over to my old man's pad and kick back by the pool for a while. He and my step mom won't care."

Wayne calmed a little and looked at Alan as Debbie went to help Jessie up. "Yeah, you're right. You two are done, so we might as well get the hell out of here."

The group stared at each other before collecting their belongings and heading out the door with Jessie in tow. She felt relieved to be heading home, but didn't cherish the idea of riding all that way with Wayne.

All four stepped onto the rickety porch and started for their cars.

"Where the fuck do you think you're going?" Wayne asked Jessie as she walked toward the Beamer. He continued to wipe the blood from his mouth. "Get another ride home, bitch."

Alan and Debbie now stopped, watching intently as they readied to enter the SUV.

"Stop fooling around, Wayne," Jessie yelled. "Just get me home, okay?"

"Go fuck yourself. You're not coming with me. Start walking."

Jessie froze, not knowing what to do. She looked frantically at Debbie and Alan.

"That's enough, you guys," Debbie finally interjected. "Wayne, if you're not going to take her, she can ride with us."

Jessie started toward the SUV only to be shoved away by an approaching Alan. "Nah, I don't think so. No one disses my bro and gets away with it." Before Debbie could interrupt, he swung around to her and said, "And don't you say a goddamn word if you know what's good for ya. Just get in the car and shut the fuck up, or we'll let you foot it out of here too."

He shot Wayne a look and the two friends smiled, pounding their fists together.

Wayne then added, "Know your place, Debbie, or I'll ruin your rep just like I'm going to do to this bitch when we get back to school."

Debbie now sat obediently in the SUV, head bowed, with tears streaming from her eyes. She avoided making eye contact with Jessie but kept mouthing, "I am so sorry, Jessie, I am so sorry."

"If you make it out of here alive, I'll consider giving you another chance," Wayne yelled in laughter as he jumped in his car, started it up, and pulled away.

Jessie took two steps and then froze. She stood alone in the dark with tears in her eyes, watching the glimmer of red tail lights slowly disappearing down the dirt road and into the darkness.

CHAPTER

33

A mixture of fear and anger now gripped Jessie. She stood unmoving in the night, not knowing what to do as the murmur of the engines faded into the distance. Being trapped in the swampy underbrush at night, or anytime for that matter, was not a scenario one would wish on anyone.

God, please help me. I can't believe this is happening to me.

Jessie took a few more steps before stopping at the sound of a growing rumble.

Engines, I hear engines. They must be coming back to get me!

Yeah, he taught me a lesson, I'll shut my mouth. I'm still not sleeping with the jerk, but he scared the shit out of me enough not to come out here again.

After a second she realized the sounds were different from the cars that had left a few minutes ago.

Terror took hold of Jessie, now caught in the sweep of head-lights as a pair of quads emerged from the darkness. She ran into the woods to avoid the lights while they rolled to a stop in front of the shack.

* * *

"I saw a girl take off that way!" The shout from one operative rang in the air as he dismounted his quad and secured his rifle.

The other quickly dismounted and ran into the shack.

"Shit, there was someone here. There's empty beer cans and you can still smell the pot. Damn it, find them now!" bellowed the man exiting the shack.

Both men removed their flashlights and started canvassing the area.

"Fuck, we're screwed if someone was here. Trout will have us skinned for using this shack," fumed Jack.

"I wouldn't worry about Trout," Jesus answered. "The WWS doesn't take things like this lightly. We'll be gator food if they find out."

* * *

Jessie Anderson huddled between two bushes, ankle deep in muck as she hid from the intruders.

Tears streamed down her cheeks as she tried to muffle her sobs, watching the two men circle the area looking for her. Within fif-teen feet to her left, Jessie heard a noise behind her and turned to see a huge alligator sitting quietly with gleaming red eyes.

CHAPTER

34

"Doug? So that's the alias you've been going by?" The elderly man, head of the Coastal Access group, grinned as the two men sat abreast of each other. The Town Car slipped quietly out of downtown Melbourne and headed north along the river.

Doug sat solemnly, staring straight ahead before finally speaking. "Judge, long time no see. Sorry to see you still seem to be in good health. Maybe we'll all get lucky, and sooner rather than later the Grim Reaper will put a scythe up your ass."

The old man only smiled, tapping his cane on the floor board between his legs.

"See you're as big a prick now as when I first met your ugly ass all those years ago." The Judge sounded amused.

Doug sat and glared at him from the corner of his eye.

"I actually have to give you credit," the Judge continued. "I never thought you'd have the balls to bring your pathetic ass back to Florida."

Doug didn't acknowledge the dig.

The Judge raised his cane as if threatening him. "You ran out of here like a puppy dog with your tail between your legs. You didn't have the balls to stand up and fight for what you believe. I thought you'd hide in that cesspool called New Jersey forever."

Doug finally looked at the Judge.

"Yes, I've known where you were all along. I always have, and I'd have left you alone if you stayed dead and above the Mason-Dixon Line."

Doug finally spoke. "You really think I stayed away because I was scared of you? Please don't flatter yourself. I'd have killed you in a heartbeat if I had the chance. I knew if you couldn't get to me, you'd leave my family alone."

The bodyguard turned and looked at Doug as the Town Car continued to slide along Riverside Drive.

Doug dismissed the thug's stare. "No, old man, my family is more important than you. Their safety came first. That's why I left."

The Judge replied with a girlish chuckle, "Really now, you weren't too worried about safety when you let your brother sail alone down the river. That boating accident was meant for both of you. But I think you already know that by now. Everyone was led to believe you were on it, well played. But we know better now, don't we...Doug? You knew of the danger and high-tailed it out of here."

"Fuck you, you low life. Go screw yourself."

The Judge laughed. "Screw myself? Yeah, okay, cowboy. It's bad enough I've had to fuck your drunken ex-wife all these years. She was a good lay for a while, when I first took her away from you."

Doug became solemn again. His jaw tightened, but he forced himself to speak. "Don't flatter yourself; she wasn't attracted to the three inches between your legs. She lost sight of life and thought the prestige of being a politician's wife meant more than her family."

"Ah, it's nice to see you still have feelings for her. The next time she's drunk and unconscious and I'm on top of her pounding away, I'll remember to say hi for ya,"

Doug sat back and looked out the window at the palms and homes of his hometown as they went whizzing by. It was still a beautiful, magical place to Doug. He missed all the wonderful years of memories, in a time that was now long gone.

"Well," the Judge began with a smile, "by showing up, you made completing my project a lot easier. It's a plan I've long had in the works, and you'd even find it ingenious. You and your asshole son are the last two pieces to the puzzle. Sorry to say you'll never see it when I complete it. But I can promise you one thing, you'll be meeting that Grim Reaper way before I do."

The two sat in silence as the car neared its destination.

CHAPTER

35

Tucker found himself not standing on a dune or beach as in his previous dreams, but on a knoll in the middle of a vast marshland. A light, misty rain fell as he surveyed the area. He had a sense of familiarity about the place, but from where? He had no idea or any reason to explain why he would be at this location.

In the distance, a figure appeared as the rain abated and an orange moon rose on the eastern horizon. The silhouette wasn't clear at first. It took on a myriad of colors, and its shape changed more than once. It was small, then long, wider, then small again as the apparition began to take shape. Tucker was mesmerized as the collection of colors morphed until a figure finally formed.

An Indian now approached him. Standing in a canoe, head bowed with outstretched arms, Tucker recognized his great-uncle

Osci from their previous meetings as he drifted up the canal toward him.

"My nephew," Osci said as he raised his eyes to meet Tucker's. "You, my son, are the embodiment of me, we share the same soul."

Tucker answered, "Yes, Great-uncle, I have grown to understand that. I have completed all you wished, and the guilty ones family has been punished for the long ago murder of your child. I'm not sure what else you want from me."

Osci stared hard. "Remember, family ties bind us beyond time and space. Our souls are forever one, my son. What I have experienced, so have you, my son."

Tucker looked around and realized it was the area where the two murdered teens were found.

Tucker said, "My uncle, this land we are now in, it is so familiar to me, yet until the other day, I knew I had never been here."

The apparition stared at Tucker as warmth emanated from its center and washed over him. Osci's long, dark hair swayed in the shimmering heat, his dark eyes focused on Tucker.

"You have been here. This is the land of your ancestors," Osci said as he stretched his arms out toward the vast wetlands. "When you experience the feeling of déjà vu, it is because you are familiar with an event or surrounding from the past, the past of the soul connected to you. It is that way for all people, but only some allow themselves to feel the connection." Osci lifted his hands toward the heavens.

"You wonder why I have again come to you. I am here to give you a message. I am here to warn you that men have come to take our land from us and destroy its resources. Your nana has tried to make you understand, but I am here now to explain."

The mention of Nana caught him by surprise.

"Yes, Uncle, I have seen Nana, but I haven't had any communications with her."

"And you shall not!" Osci thundered.

"Great-Uncle, I had a dream recently, one about my nana, but I could not understand what she wanted."

The Indian answered, "You are not connected with your nana; she cannot communicate with you. Her soul is connected to another. You and I are one. I have come to tell you that you are the one to protect our land. It is your land, the land of our people." The apparition looked at Tucker before continuing. "You have the power, as before, through the written word to stop it. Many have lost their lives over this land. Your father and his brother included."

The last sentence caught Tucker by surprise. "My father's brother? Uncle, my father was an only child. I don't understand."

"Your father's brother," he repeated, "was murdered many years ago on the water. Your father has now passed on too, as a result of his interest in our land. You are also in danger. Let it be written. This is the sacred land of our family, and no one will defile it."

The apparition slowly faded, and to Tucker's left, at the base of the knoll, a large alligator with glowing red eyes appeared. Eyes that remained fixed on Tucker.

The gator slowly turned, tucked its head, and slid into the water.

Tucker stood more confused than ever. How was this land his land, and why didn't anyone ever tell him about his uncle?

These questions swirled around in Tucker's mind as he drifted back into a deep sleep.

CHAPTER

36

"Your daughter is attempting to reach you on your cellular device...Your daughter is attempting to reach you on your cellular device..."

The message resounding from my phone woke me from my slumber. As I reached for the cell, I looked around, disoriented. It took me a few seconds to finally realize I was in my new condo and not on the yacht I had grown accustomed to. I had fallen asleep after bringing my belongings over from the marina. The clock registered 12:30 as I answered.

"Daddy...ohmigod," came the barely audible voice of Jessie as I struggled to clear my head. "Daddy, I'm scared. I don't know where I am, and there are men with guns..."

The word *guns* woke me up. "Jessie, hold on, honey. Now calm down and tell me what's going on."

"I'm...I'm...I'm not sure. I was with Wayne and he...he...left me," she said between sobs.

My head exploded. *That fucking kid, I knew he was no goddamn good. I'll kill that son-of-a-bitch if he's done anything to hurt my daughter.*

"Calm down. Take a deep breath and slowly tell me what's going on," I said, taking a second to compose myself as I pulled on my sweats, slipped on my sneakers, and headed for the door.

Silence fell over the phone before Jessie finally whispered, "I was with Wayne. He took me out into the brush, out past I-95 in Cocoa. It was supposed to be a party, but no one was here, and because I wouldn't...wouldn't..."

I cut in. "That's okay, baby, don't worry about that now, just tell me where you are."

She continued, a little calmer, "He left me here. That asshole just left me, and there are men...they saw me. They're looking for me."

A thousand thoughts ran through my mind in a matter of seconds. *What was going on? That kid Wayne and men with guns; what had he gotten Jessie into? I'd take care of that fuck when I got my hands on him.* But I could take care of that later. I now needed to concentrate on my daughter.

"Okay, Jessie, listen. I need you to stay right where you are," I said, grabbing my keys and running out the door. "Stay away from those men and anyone else you don't know. We have no idea who they are or what they're up to out there at this time of night. Now try and remember what road you were on. You said you drove out from Cocoa past I-95. That was probably Route 520."

"Oh, Daddy, I think that was it, but I'm not sure. We made a left off Tropical Trail onto the main road before the Home Depot and then passed under 95, like I said."

In my mind I could now envision the route they took. It was on the same road the poor teens from Texas were found murdered.

Anxiety started to set in. It would take me a good thirty minutes, at a high rate of speed, to reach that area.

"Baby, how far on 520 did you travel?"

"I don't know, Daddy. I remember making a left somewhere out here. I didn't pay attention." Her whisper could barely be heard.

I jumped in my Jeep and headed over the causeway to grab I-95 North, the quickest way to Route 520.

"Jessie, where are you right now, this second?"

"I told you, Daddy, somewhere off that road I told you about. Didn't you hear me the first time?" she wept.

"No, Jessie. I mean physically. You, at this moment."

"I'm in some bushes, with muck up to my ankles, hiding from those men."

"Okay, stay there, calm down, and don't move a muscle. Stay as quiet as possible," I told her, keeping my voice level low hoping to compose her. I didn't want her to bolt and run. The idea of her being in the swamp was something I didn't want to think about. Besides the two men, alligators, panthers, water moccasins, and black widow spiders inhabited the area. Then an idea hit me.

"Jessie, can you see those men anywhere nearby?"

"No, Daddy. They went in different directions."

I glanced out the window at the clear, starlit night as I streaked toward the highway.

"Okay, honey. Just 'cause they're not around doesn't mean they won't be back. So stay extremely quiet and still."

"Daddy, I'm so scared." Jessie continued to softly cry.

"Jessie, everything is going to be okay," I said with my fingers crossed. Please God, don't make me a liar. "Your cell is an iPhone, isn't it?"

"Yes."

"Now listen to what I want you to do. I want you to find your map application that came with the phone."

"I have so many apps, Daddy, I—"

I interrupted her. "Just find it. The thing came with your phone."

Silence for a few seconds before she answered. "Got it, Dad. Now what?"

"Okay, good. Now follow my directions and everything will be fine."

I hit the entrance ramp to the interstate and accelerated.

"Tap the app and open it."

"Okay, done. But Daddy, it now says I only have twenty percent battery life left."

Shit, I thought. "No big deal, honey," I lied. "I'll be there shortly. Now type in Desoto Parkway for me in the start section of the directions list."

"Why, Dad? I'm not at Desoto."

"Will you just follow my directions?" I hissed.

After a momentary pause she was back. "Okay, Daddy. I see a red pin and a green pin on the map that came up. Wow, that's pretty cool."

"Great, Jessie. See, I told you I'd find you." My daughter was stuck in a dangerous situation but still found the time to think something she just discovered on her phone was cool. "The green pin is Desoto and you are the red one. On the bottom right of the screen is an icon like a sheet of paper. Tap it."

"All done. It says 'route overview.'"

"Fantastic, honey. You can copy the list of directions and text them to me."

"Okay, Daddy, but the warning message just came on and said I now have only ten percent power left."

"Just send me the directions, and then we'll conserve the battery."

She sent me the directions. She was right about the route Wayne had taken. The iPhone map also had her off of Route 532, a left about two miles past the murder scene.

"Got it, Jessie, great. Now listen to me carefully."

"Okay, Daddy."

"Follow my directions to a T. I want you to sit as quiet as you can. Not a sound. If those men come back, lie in the muck and bury your face. We don't want the moonlight to reflect off your face."

"Got it, Daddy."

"Now when we hang up, I want you to power off your phone to save energy and—"

"But Daddy, I want to talk to you." She started to sob harder.

"Stop it now," I demanded. "Do as you're told. I have a good idea where you are. When I get near, I'll start blowing my horn. When you hear it, power your phone back up. Got it?"

"Yes, I got it."

I approached the exit for Route 520 and Cocoa. "I'll see you in about fifteen minutes. Love you. Now power off."

"Love you too, Daddy. Hurry up," she said and then the phone fell silent.

I headed west and quickly dialed Craig.

"Hi, this is Craig," came the response. "Sorry I'm unable to come to the phone at the moment, but if you leave your name and number...oh, wait, I have your number on here...I'll call you back as soon as I can."

"Shit," I yelled into the cell phone.

CHAPTER

37

"Where the fuck is that girl?" Jesus snarled as he and Jack swung their flashlights from side to side over the marshland.

"Damn it. She must have swung around in the other direction," Jack replied. He stared into the darkness with his rifle cocked and ready, flashlight now focused on Jesus. "When we find her, we'll have to dispose of the body deeper in the woods where no one will ever find her."

Jesus shaded his eyes. "Get that fucking thing out of my face, and we're not disposing of anything. Don't you remember what Trout told us?"

Jack snapped the flashlight off as Jesus drew closer. "We'll find her, tell her we're hunters, and get her to the main road. What happens then will be out of our control."

Jack stared at him. "Really? Hunters? And when she tells the Florida Fish and Wildlife Service officers, they'll show up to start combing the area looking for us and stumble on Area 176. That'll go over real well."

Jesus had no answer as Jack continued, "So screw Trout. You want the WWS to find out we breached security and used the shack as our own? If you remember, we were supposed to eradicate any and all signs of life havin' been in that cabin. If you want to take the hit for that, be my guest. You deal with the consequences. I don't feel like being turned into fish chum and spewed all over Sebastian Inlet."

Jesus knew Jack was right. They would have to find the kid, dispose of the body, and remove any trace of human existence from the cabin and surrounding area. Having to deal with the wrath of the organization was not a pleasant prospect.

"We'll start at the cabin and circle back," Jack said, taking command of the situation. "Start at the north end and head clockwise around the perimeter. I'll do the same from the opposite direction and deal with the deeper part of the marsh."

The two operatives agreed and synchronized their watches. "We should rendezvous back here by oh-two-hundred," continued Jack as he started the search.

Jesus clicked on his flashlight with a sweeping motion as he moved along the perimeter.

The moon, which had shone brightly till now, disappeared behind the evening storm clouds that seemed to pop up from nowhere.

Damn, Jesus thought to himself as he glanced at the sky. *I thought they called for a clear, starlit night. Those weathermen are assholes. The only profession that can be wrong half the time and never lose their job.*

* * *

Jessie knelt, wrapping her arms around her legs to ward off the evening chill the marshland was known for. She closed her eyes and slowly started counting, hoping by the time she neared one thousand her dad would be near.

Please, Daddy, get here soon.

The sound of breaking twigs startled her from her trance. A large beam of light swung from side to side as a figure loomed nearby. Jessie slid a little deeper into the brush and buried her face in her arms. The beam of light swung past her, stopped, and returned. "Oh God. Please, Daddy, where are you?" she whispered.

Jessie raised her head, peered over her crossed arms, and saw a figure approaching to within fifteen feet of her left. The beam of light froze as Jessie heard a voice.

"Holy shit. What the—" A shriek pierced the night air.

Jessie froze in terror. Beside her, an enormous alligator shook its head from side to side as it slowly made its way into deeper water. She watched in disbelief as the beast turned and looked back at her. Yes, at her, with gleaming red eyes.

Just then, a car horn sounded in the distance. She turned on her phone.

CHAPTER

38

"I can hear you, Daddy. You're very close. Hurry, please hurry." Jessie's voice rang in my ear as I raced along the main road looking for the entrance to the woods where Wayne had left my daughter. I had sped past an entrance a short while back that headed into the underbrush, but it was so muddy and bumpy I knew a Beamer could never have been able to enter. I continued to speed along Route 532 looking for anything a small vehicle like his could have navigated.

I rounded a small curve and spotted a clearing in the woods. A "No Trespassing" sign and a small open gate welcomed me. I made a hard left and banged my Jeep down the easement onto a gravel road that led into the brush.

"Jessie, can you still hear me?" I yelled into the cell.

"Yes, Daddy, you're getting louder. I can see your lights through the trees."

"Okay, honey. Stay to the side. When I get near, wave me down. Jessie? Jessie?" Her phone went dead.

I hit the speed dial on my phone for Craig and gave him directions. He and another deputy were five miles behind and closing fast. I had finally reached him earlier, and in an instant he was on his way. He lived closer to the area, just off Tropical Trail, so he didn't have far to travel.

I continued down a well-worn dirt road, avoiding the few ruts that created a rocky ride when hit. Trees along the overgrown path grew denser before opening up to the flat marshland.

A hand up ahead waved frantically, and I jolted to a stop. I was out of the car before it stopped. Jessie ran into my arms and wept.

"It's okay, honey. I'm here."

She stammered, "Daddy, Daddy...it was awful. An alligator... men with guns. I thought...I thought I was..."

She buried her head in my chest as I quickly guided her into the passenger seat of my car.

"Okay, Jessie. Everything is okay. Take a deep breath. There you go. That's my girl. Easy now," I said as she laid her head on my shoulder.

"I'm so sorry for being out here," she sobbed. "I should have known better."

"Don't worry about that now. I'm just happy you're safe. Now tell me what happened."

We huddled together, in the middle of nowhere, under the dome light of my Jeep as she composed herself. "Wayne left me here." Her voice still cracked. "There was supposed to be a party, but no one was here...well, another couple was, and he wanted to have...he wanted..."

"Don't worry about that," I said. "Who were the men with guns?"

"There were two of them. They saw me and were looking for me. That's when I called you. Then when one got close to me, an alligator grabbed him and dragged him into the water. I was so scared."

I sat and listened to her story, while looking for any unusual movements in the darkness before saying, "They're gone now. You're out in the swamps. Everything is scary out here, and gators are all around. He probably ran into it as it was coming out of the water—"

She cut me off. "No, Daddy. Why it was so scary, Daddy, is that the alligator only grabbed him a few feet away from me. The gator must have been there all along."

"Things happen for a reason," I said.

"I guess you're right. But you know what was strange? The alligator looked right at me. It had strange red eyes that gleamed."

I just stared ahead of me into the darkness as shivers ran down my spine, and I whispered, "Thank you, Osci."

CHAPTER

39

A hundred yards from the unknown vehicle, Jack stood off to the side, hidden by shadows, with his semi-automatic cradled across his chest. He slowly crept forward to get a better view of the auto's occupants.

Where the hell is Jesus? was the immediate thought that entered his mind. They were too close to the end of their mission to let events spiral out of control.

Trout won't like it, but he'll thank us later for taking care of the situation. And where the fuck is Jesus?

Jack continued moving forward, finally able to see two people sitting inside the Jeep Cherokee. Approaching from the driver's side would give him the best chance for a direct kill, and with the driver eliminated, the passenger would be easy prey. Even if she got out and ran, she wouldn't get far. Then he'd drive the Jeep and the bodies into the deepest recesses of the marsh, where no one would ever find any trace of their existence.

Where the hell is that guy?

Jack used the shadows created by the scrub pines and cloud cover to conceal himself as he maneuvered to within twenty yards of his objective. After closely assessing the situation, he decided to move to point blank range and use his sidearm rather than the rifle to make the kill. He crouched and slowly approached the lit cabin of the Jeep. Both occupants sat quietly in discussion, with the female laying her head on the male's shoulder. Jack, now within ten feet of the door, drew his weapon, took aim, and froze.

Sirens grew louder as Jack saw the flashing red and blue lights of two sheriff's office cruisers rumbling toward them through the woods.

Shit! What the hell?

Aborting the kill, Jack dropped his weapon to his side and disappeared into the shadows.

CHAPTER
40

I left the area and headed back to Honeymoon Lake with Jessie safely at my side. Craig and another deputy remained at the scene to take a closer look at the abandoned shack before heading back to their station. The dashboard clock now gleamed three in the morning.

I punched in the number of my ex-wife and patiently waited for her to answer.

"Yes, Tucker. This better be good. Do you have any idea what time it is, or are you drunk again with nothing better to do?"

What a lovely greeting. "Morning, Marion, I know what time it is. To answer your question, no, I'm not drunk. But I was just wondering if you could wake Jessie and put her on the phone for me. She didn't pick up her cell when I called."

"Seriously now, you're kidding me, right? You called me at this hour to talk to your daughter? Well, she's not here. I guess she'll call you back when she gets the chance. Go back to bed, Tucker," she mumbled as she started to hang up the phone.

"Hold on, Marion," I interjected. "By chance do you know where she is tonight?" I smiled as I looked at my daughter sleeping in the passenger seat while turning the corner and heading south on Tropical Trail.

"Of course I do, you idiot. I'm her mother, aren't I? She and that lovely boy, Wayne, were going to a party in Cocoa, at another friend's house. Then she went over to her girlfriend Connie's for a sleep-over with a few other girls from school."

"Oh, that's wonderful. I'm glad you got a chance to check this out with the other parents. Did you get a chance to talk to her tonight?"

"No, Tucker. She's a big girl and can take care of herself. Plus the nice kids she's finally associating with gives me nothing to worry about. If you were any kind of father, you'd know. So, Tucker, is there anything else you want to bother me with? I need to get back to sleep."

I was ready to explode. Steam was blowing out of my ears, but nothing would get accomplished at this point by losing my cool. I kept my composure.

"Well, tell you what, Marion. I'm on Tropical right now and will be there in a few minutes. I have Jessie with me. She was abandoned by your wonderful Wayne in a remote area out past I-95. If you were any kind of mother, you'd know."

I clicked off the phone and reached over to stroke my daughter's hair. Memories flooded back to a time when she was a toddler and rode with me, just happy to be with Daddy. I let my hand drop to her shoulder as I made the turn onto her street. She stirred for the moment and whispered, "Love you, Daddy."

"We're almost home, baby."

I continued up the palm-lined street and made a left into her driveway. Marion and Charles were standing at the door waiting as I pulled to a stop in front of the garage.

I shook Jessie. "We're home." My teenage daughter looked at me and smiled as her mother reached for the passenger door and flung it open.

Marion uttered, "Jessie, oh my God, sweetheart." She helped her from the car as tears welled up in her eyes. "How could you have let this happen?"

Our daughter stood there covered in mud up to her knees, with dirty, matted hair strewn across her shoulders, and started to cry. "Really Mother? Really?"

"Marion, now is not the time," came the unexpected remark from Charles as I stepped around the Jeep. Our eyes locked.

I began quietly, "Marion, Charles is right. Now is not the time and place for this. Jessie's okay. That's all that matters, but you better check into that Wayne character and his friends. I know..." I emphasized, "he's not the type of young man you'd want your daughter to be around."

She stared at me, and for once in her life had no comment to throw back. Charles just looked at me. His eyes told me we were on the same page.

"Jessie, I'm going to head home now. You get some rest and I'll talk to you tomorrow."

She ran to me and flung her arms around my neck and again said, "Love you, Daddy," as she started to cry and raced toward the door with Marion in her wake. I turned and walked toward the driver' side.

"Tucker, I just want to say…" Charles had begun to speak, but stopped. He didn't need to say another word as we nodded to each other and smiled.

I got into the Jeep, backed down the driveway, and set my sights for Satellite Beach. The homes on Honeymoon Lake faded from my rearview mirror.

CHAPTER
41

I had a restless night, with little sleep from running the previous evening's events through my mind. Karla not being there also added to my agitation. But I was up, showered, and out of the condo before my alarm went off. It was just one night, and I already felt at home in my new surroundings.

I stopped for my coffee at Dunkin' Donuts, near Satellite High, and waited in line with a group of teenagers as they jockeyed for position, wanting their morning caffeine jolt to prepare them for school.

I wondered, as I watched the kids fooling around, how many of the girls could have been caught in a similar situation as my daughter. On the surface, they all looked fine, but how many were harboring the secrets that many teens conceal? We hear so much about bullying in school, but people forget to mention their constant struggle with peer pressure.

We condition them to grow up way too fast, I thought as a young couple walked out with the male's hand on the female's ass, holding on for a little squeeze.

I paid for my coffee, left my change in the tip jar, and headed north on A1A before making a left, and drove west over the Pineda Causeway.

Looking in the rearview mirror, I marveled at the colors of the morning sun as it peeked with golden rays over the horizon.

I swung right on US1 and reached the office before most people were awake. I walked into the building, passed the empty steel desks, and flicked on the lights to my office.

Taking a seat at my desk and situating my coffee and donut… okay, two donuts…perfectly within reach, I powered up my computer and patiently waited, taking a bite of my French cruller. The computer hummed to life, and the screen finally popped up for me to sign in. I punched in my password, and voilà, within seconds I was instantly connected to the rest of the planet via the World Wide Web.

Sitting back in my chair and sipping on my now lukewarm coffee, I saw that my mail icon was flickering in the right corner as a number of messages awaited my attention.

Only a few of the senders interested me; the first was labeled "US Globe Article," and the sender was L. Greenwood.

Who the heck is L. Greenwood? was my initial thought before realizing she was the woman who had interviewed me a while back.

"Dear Mr. Anderson," the e-mail began. "I hope this letter finds you and your family, past and present, doing well."

Oh shit, this is going to be interesting.

"I have attached my final revision of our interview for your early viewing. I hope you like the article I have attached; it's going to be printed in next week's issue. I look forward to hearing from you in the near future. Yours in journalism, L. Greenwood."

"Yours in journalism?" Yeah, okay, she writes for a gossip rag and I, well, I'm at least a realist. I'm no more a journalist than the guy next door. But if anything else, I'm at least honest with myself. I had been more than lucky in my profession, and lately things just seemed to fall in place for me. At least that had been the case this past year.

I smiled at the word *journalist* and clicked on the highlighted download option next to the word "attachment."

The article, to my surprise, was very well written and in no way made a mockery of my experiences, as I thought it would. Ms. Greenwood simply stated the facts and left it up to the readers to decide for themselves whether or not they believed my story and about my connection to the afterlife and spirits.

I was pleasantly surprised with what I read and sent Greenwood an e-mail thanking her for her professionalism.

Just then, a new message appeared. The subject read "Coastal Access." Seeing that name again caught me totally by surprise. I checked to see who the sender was, and again I couldn't locate one. I tried a quick trace but was unsuccessful in finding the origination of the URL address.

The last time I received something labeled "Coastal Access," the e-mail simply read, "It's all about Coastal Access," and gave no further information. But this one looked different.

The e-mail began: "Coastal Access – follow the links." Under the sentence, only a click away, several links were illuminated in blue.

The first link took me to an aerial map view of a wooden landscape; the area looked to be between Route 520 and 532. And that was it: no words, description, or explanation. Nothing unusual jumped out at me about the area, but after looking carefully, I finally noticed two marks on the map. One was the same location where I had been frantically searching for Jessie last night, and the other mark showed the murder location of the Texas teens. I hadn't realized their close proximity. I would have never tied the two together, but now I couldn't help but wonder.

I couldn't wait to back out and hit on link number two. When I did, I wasn't surprised at all; it was no big deal, just the article I wrote last year about political crime in our area. Again no added explanation for the reference to that article, but why send it to me?

Now the third link. As soon as the old newspaper article emerged on the screen, the hairs on the back of my neck stood up. It was the photo and article my grandmother had kept hidden from me for so many years and the graphic photo and information of my father's boat explosion.

Was this some kind of sick joke? Who would do this? Who knew about the murders and the area my daughter was stranded in? Why bring up the past? I had so many questions now, but clearly, without identifying the sender, I wasn't going to get the answers I wanted. It was time to do a little research of my own. My dad's death, the article on Judge Arnold Galley's corruption, and the aerial map from the other night had something in common, but what? I needed to find out.

The e-mail merely ended with, "I'll be in touch. More information to follow." What the hell did that mean, and when would it follow, days, weeks, months? I now needed a road trip.

I picked up my cell, grabbed my coffee, and headed back out to my car.

"Hey, buddy, you're here early," rang the familiar voice of my boss, Mitch. "Where you headed off to in such a hurry?"

I paused for a moment, thinking about how much I wanted to say. "Oh, hey there, Mitch, I'm just heading out to meet Craig, thought I'd check out the area where those kids were murdered. Craig is being nice enough to let me tag along." I didn't dare mention Jessie's experience. I knew I'd never get out of the office if I did.

"Okay, keep me in the loop." Mitch's voice trailed off as he disappeared around the corner.

Okay, so I lied. Craig wasn't really going to meet me. I was heading to the old shack and marsh area to start my own investigation. I needed to look deeper into what these e-mails represented and the connections they might have with each other. If I thought I'd need help, I'd reach out to Craig, but that could wait.

I jumped into my Jeep and steered a path for Route 523. The question kept bursting in my head. *Who the hell is sending me this Coastal Access shit, and what does it all mean?*

CHAPTER

42

"What do you mean you can't find Jesus?" growled the cracking voice of Colonel Trout. "How the hell could you lose your partner? Where's your bullshit military slogan now? Never leave a man behind, my ass."

"Sir," Jack answered, "we had a major incident last night."

Trout just stood there, the blood draining from his face. "Oh shit," he mouthed, sinking down into the chair behind his desk.

"Take a seat, Jack. And tell me what the fuck happened."

"Sir, we had a possible imminent threat to the security of Area 176." Jack paused as he sat down across from the colonel.

"Go on," Trout encouraged, clenching his jaw.

"We had a group of teenagers in the northern quadrant—"

"Please don't tell me you killed more teenagers?" Trout interrupted.

"No, sir, we were following your instructions. There was a small group of them, and we scared them off. They appeared to leave but left one of their own behind. We, Jesus and I, started to search the area. As we went in different directions, a vehicle came back to retrieve the girl."

"A girl? You're telling me you had a girl running loose in the underbrush?"

"Yes, sir. But as I was saying, she was picked up and removed from the area before we could reach her." Jack was careful not to mention she was picked up by a different car than the one she arrived in, along with two police vehicles.

"Fuck me," Trout said, trying to keep his composure. "So this girl was collected and all parties removed themselves from the area. Is that correct?"

"Yes, sir," Jack answered.

"So what the fuck happened to Jesus?"

"That's just it, Colonel, I don't know. We both circled the perimeter to locate the intruder. As I said, she was picked up and removed before we reached her. I rendezvoused at the assigned spot, but Jesus never showed. I waited at least three hours for him."

"Did you hear any altercation? And don't bullshit me," Trout demanded, raising his voice.

"No, sir, no one knew we were even there."

"Okay, this is too fucking strange. It's not like he could just dis-appear into thin air."

The colonel rocked back and forth in his chair, rubbing his hand across his crew cut while Jack sat in silence.

"How about his quad?" Trout asked.

"I recovered that, sir. Everything was intact, just as Jesus left it."

Both men looked at each other.

"Okay, Jack. I want you to head out there and retrace your steps. It's light out now. He couldn't have gone far. Maybe he became disoriented and lost. Fell and hit his head. Anything could have happened. Has he been sick or acting strange of late?"

Jack paused for a second, apparently deep in thought. "Now that you mention it, sir, he has been acting a little strange."

"Well, go ahead, spit it out."

"He's been saying some weird stuff, about seeing Indians."

"Indians?" Trout sounded astonished.

"Yes, sir, an Indian. A few times he told me about seeing him. He seems to think one is out there, in the marsh, following him."

"And did you see this so-called Indian in the woods?"

"Me? No, sir."

"Have you two been drinking or smoking anything? You know I gave you a direct order to stop that shit."

Jack's voice rose, as if the suggestion was insulting. "No, sir, we do not partake in the vile nature of drugs and alcohol anymore, of course, at your request."

Trout grimaced at Jack from the corner of his eye. *Yeah, okay,* he thought to himself. *You both were hooked on some scary shit in Central America, so don't try and act like you two don't indulge. We both know that's a load of crap.*

He remained calm. "Okay, head back out. If you don't find him I'll call Andrews up from the southern sector to assist you. Radio me in an hour. Now get out of my face."

Jack stood, saluted, and removed himself from the command center.

Holy shit, the colonel thought. *These fucking guys are killing me.* He took a pink bottle of "stomach chalk," as he called it, from his drawer and slugged down two gulps to quiet the rumbling in his stomach.

Just then the phone rang.

"Trout!" came the shout from the other end. "What the fuck is going on out there?"

"Nothing, everything is status quo, sir. I'm not sure what you're talking about," he answered, crossing his fingers in hopes of not receiving a surprise visit from his superior.

"Bullshit, Trout, don't you fucking lie to me. A report just crossed my desk filed by a sheriff's officer last night. The report details a call they responded to in our northern section. Do I have to come out there myself and straighten this crap out?"

Trout simmered in silence, squeezing the skin between his eyes with his thumb and forefinger. *Shit*, he thought to himself.

He finally spoke. "Sir, everything here is secure, I can assure you. I'll go out personally and double check the area myself and see if anything happened."

"You do that, Trout. I want a full report back to me by eighteen hundred hours. We're lucky I have an inside operative stationed at the Titusville barracks. He quickly intercepted it for us. We'd be shit out of luck if the police started snooping around." The line went dead.

Trout slowly put the receiver down and rose from his desk. He stood for a moment, allowing the blood to flow to his head again, before grabbing his hat and sunglasses and stepping to the trailer's door. He turned the knob, pushed, and paused on the top step before stepping down.

I'm royally fucked. Intruders, a missing operative, and now an Indian. What the hell did I get myself into?

CHAPTER

43

My coffee was cold, but I still carried the container with me, sipping it as I approached my Jeep. Even though the air had a tinge of coolness, the warmth of the morning sun felt good warming my face. I slipped into the driver's seat and strapped in as my cell phone rang out the familiar tag for Karla.

"Morning, hope you slept well without the snoring bear," I teased, firing up the engine, getting ready to go.

"Hi, honey," she said with a laugh. "Yeah, I slept well, but I really missed my big teddy."

We both laughed at how childish we sounded. I placed my coffee in its holder and switched the cell to speaker, heading north on US 1.

"How'd the autopsy go on the two teens?" I asked, then realized it was a bad idea to ask over the phone. I could sense by Karla's awkward silence that she knew better than to answer. With the history of having my phone tapped and monitored, we knew any breach of confidentiality from her end could lead to her dismissal.

I quickly changed my tone before she could answer. "We'll have a nice, quiet dinner and replay the day's events when you get off. Sound good?"

"That sounds great," she chimed. "I'll bring a bottle of wine, as long as you do the cooking."

"Not a problem. You got a deal, as long as you do the dishes," I added with a chuckle.

"Dishes?" Karla answered. "With the way you cook? You're the only person I know who uses almost every utensil possible when making something. But okay, honey, it's a deal. I'll throw in a few paper plates to make my life a little easier."

I laughed, knowing the paper plates would get her out of cleaning up, but that was okay; my cooking consisted of take-out from the Texas Road House.

Karla continued, "Oh, I forgot to ask. Did the furniture arrive yet?"

"No, should be later today. They gave me a window between two and four. My upstairs neighbor was nice enough to say he'd let them in for me. I gave him a twenty and another twenty for the delivery guys if they drop the stuff in the places I mapped out."

"You left a map?" She laughed aloud sarcastically.

"Yeah, what's wrong with that? Better than me pushing everything around and breaking a sweat."

Karla continued to laugh. "You're priceless."

I still didn't get what was so funny, but whatever.

"Okay, I'll see you around six?" I asked.

"Six sounds good. I'll see you tonight then, love ya."

I hung up the phone and quickly speed dialed Jessie.

"Hi, Daddy," Jess whispered into the phone.

"Hey, honey, you sound like you're just getting up."

"Yeah," she yawned.

"It's kinda late. You slept that long?"

"I'm just so tired and sore, Daddy."

"Yeah, I can see why. You had a rough night last night. Just hang around the house, maybe lay out by the pool for a little while and get some sun. That'll make you feel better. And Jessie, don't spend any more time thinking about..." I had a hard time saying his name, "that...that Wayne kid."

"Oh, don't worry about that, Dad. I've learned my lesson with that jerk."

"Good. You're an intelligent and beautiful young lady. You can do a lot better than him. Set your standards higher. You deserve a good guy."

"Dad, no one will ever be good enough for you, but thanks anyway."

"No need to thank me, honey, that's what I'm here for. I'll let you go now, so rest up."

With a simple click, the call ended. My little girl was growing up so fast and learning life's lessons the hard way.

I finally reached the road I was on last night, but found nothing that looked familiar. I drove for a good five minutes more, turned around, and cautiously drove along the east side of the roadway, looking for the entrance.

It has to be here.

Finally, after closely scrutinizing the ground, I found it. The difference between night and day was incredible. Last night, the access road's gate had opened up in front of me. Now it seemed to have been sucked into the foliage of Central Florida. I pulled over and exited the Jeep. The small gate that was ajar last night now had a lock and chain holding it tightly shut. A new "No Trespass-ing" sign sat on a post to the side.

I stood and thought for a minute, eying the sign, and finally decided to enter.

Ah, what the hell.

As soon as I set out on foot, I could easily tell the entrance had been tampered with. Someone had gone to extraordinary lengths, in a short period of time, to cover the roadway. There were no tire tracks as there should have been and the road was graded smooth. They had even added a few props; the old road was lightly covered with loose branches and grass clippings.

After walking about three-quarters of a mile, I was taken aback by the biggest surprise. The shack from last night was gone.

What the…I was totally shocked. I could plainly see the building was removed, but why?

"Excuse me," came a voice from over my shoulder. "You're tres-passing. This is private property." A large man in military fatigues and a rifle hanging from a strap on his shoulder appeared from nowhere.

I nearly jumped out of my skin when I heard the voice. It took a second for me to compose myself, and I nonchalantly slid my hand into my pocket and cupped my cell phone. Not knowing how to respond to the man, I quickly raised my free hand in a gesture that said, hold on a minute, and placed my cell to my ear with the other, as if I had an incoming call.

"Yes, I'm here. Yes, the same location we spoke about earlier, off of Route 532." I continued my imaginary conversation. "I know. Yeah, all right. Well, I just ran into a guy, so let me call you back when I'm leaving." I looked at the guy and smiled. "Gotcha," I said. "I'll call you back as soon as I get on the road. Okay, talk to ya in ten."

I looked at the unexpected visitor, holding the cell in my hand and hoping my fake conversation came across as legit. Seeing a guy with a rifle out in the middle of the swampland scared the shit out of me.

"Excuse me?" I said with the most surprised, congenial voice I could muster. This situation reminded me of my playing days: never let your opponent see you sweat.

"I said you're on private property."

Now come to think of it, I wasn't sure whose property this belonged to, but I wasn't in the mood to argue with a dude twice my size, holding a gun. So I took a chance and went with a different approach.

"My name is Tucker Anderson. I was hoping to find a William J. Tully. He used to hunt out of a shack around here. I thought this was the location, but I don't see his shack." I had made the name up.

The stranger answered, "There's no one out here by that name, and no shack." His eyes avoided my gaze and darted to the left. His eyes told me he was obviously lying.

"I need you, Mr. Anderson, to remove yourself from the area."

I kept my smile and slowly turned to leave. "Well, guess I'm in the wrong location. Enjoy the rest of your day." I continued to rotate my cell in my hand for him to see as I continued to walk away, nervous as hell to turn my back on a man with a gun. I walked a little farther before putting the cell up to my ear, and this time I actually did call someone…Craig.

"Hey, Craig, listen, call me back as soon as you get a chance. Remember that shack you were out at last night? Well, it's gone and some guy with a gun is out here guarding the location."

CHAPTER
44

A cold wind blew across the sea of grass. Lightning exploded all along the darkening skyline. The small canals of water rippled in wild peaks of foreboding. Tucker stood and shivered on the knoll watching thousands of apparitions scatter through the air. They were small and large. Their forms changed with each flash of light.

Tucker couldn't remember the last time he was this frightened. He shivered, not just from the chilly gusts of wind, but from the feeling of not knowing what would happen next.

From the center of the ghostly specters an alligator emerged and moved slowly toward him. As it came forward it changed numerous times until its final transformation, Osci now stood in front of Tucker and from the air summoned other spirits to his side.

The wind continued to howl and the flashes of lightning intensified. From the multitude came people he recognized: Nana,

Krystal, a man he had seen in his past but couldn't identify, and then another he recognized immediately. Doug stood in line with the rest. An explosion of noises erupted as the sky lit up and Tucker awoke.

* * *

The banging continued as I rose out of bed, pulled my sweat pants on, and walked toward the knocks on my front door.

"What is it?" Karla called out, half asleep from under the comforter. "It's three o'clock in the morning, who would be here at this hour?"

"I don't know," I said, rubbing my eyes. "You go back to sleep. I'll go check things out, probably someone at the wrong door."

I flipped on the outside light and took a look through the eyehole before slowly opening the door.

"What the hell are you doing here at this hour?" I asked Craig as he stepped inside. "You could have called me back, you didn't have to come all the way over here," I said jokingly, stifling a yawn. "Are you coming from Lou's, drunk again?"

A solemn look crossed his face.

"What?" I asked.

"Hi, Karla." Craig looked over my shoulder as she slowly appeared from the bedroom and made her way to my side, obviously curious about the early morning visit.

"Tucker, I don't know how else to say this, so I'll just blurt it out…Doug is dead."

The news shocked me awake. "He's what?"

I looked at Karla and again at Craig. Doug and I hadn't known each other that long, but we had quickly developed a close friendship.

"How? Why?"

"A couple at the marina found his body floating next to his sailboat. Our suspicions are he slipped and hit his head before rolling into the water. Maybe he was drunk or something."

"I can't believe it...he was such an accomplished seaman. He sailed up and down the East Coast as well as to the Caribbean and back."

Craig walked into the kitchen and took a seat at my pub table.

"Were there any witnesses?" I questioned Craig.

"Not as of yet. That area of the marina you guys lived in is pretty quiet and isolated."

I took a seat next to him. Karla popped open a couple of beers and brought them over to us.

Craig took a long swig. "Thanks, I needed that. Tuck, what I need you to do is come down and do a positive ID on the body. I know who he is, but you were his neighbor. I just need you to give us a positive ID."

"Sure, no problem. Let me grab a sweatshirt, and we'll be on our way."

Before I left, Craig looked at Karla. "Looks like you're not getting a break this week with all the bodies popping up all over the place."

When I returned Craig was still talking. "And may I add you look lovely at this hour of the morning."

She did look cute in nothing but a T-shirt and hair all ruffled, but she took the opportunity to flash a sneer at Craig along with her middle finger.

"Let's go," I said with a laugh, pulling my top over my head.

I gave Karla a kiss on the forehead. "Get some sleep and we'll talk later. Don't wait up for me."

"You don't have to worry about that," she yawned, but before she turned away, she squeezed my hand and said, "Sorry, Tuck."

"I'll drive," Craig said.

"No shit, use the county's gas, not mine. But I'll treat you to breakfast after we clear up this mess."

I climbed into the passenger seat and strapped in. Craig spun the car around and headed toward the morgue.

As we drove down Desoto Parkway, I decided to break the silence. "Hey, let me ask you a question. Why didn't you return my message I left you about the area we were at last night?"

"Message, what message? I never got a message from you."

I pulled my cell out and checked my recent call log. "It's right here. I called you this afternoon. You never got it?"

Craig looked at me with a measure of concern while glancing around the cruiser.

He eyed me carefully. "We'll talk at breakfast."

That's all he had to say. We sat quietly for the remainder of the ride, my curiosity now at an all-time high.

* * *

From the shadows cast by two palms and the garage complex stepped a man who had been stationed there since sundown. With Tucker gone, he now had a chance to catch a little shut-eye in his vehicle parked down the street from the condo. It wouldn't be long before he received new orders. The detective had shown up, as planned, to deliver the news about Tucker's long-lost father.

CHAPTER

45

In a large estate off South Tropical Trail, a solitary figure sat alone deep into the night and the next morning, drinking his brandy and smoking his cigar. He reviewed the files in front of him while methodically selecting a number of sheets to be swallowed up by a paper shredder sitting next to his desk.

The large study near the pool, with an excellent view of the river, was the private lair of an individual who swallowed up people much like a lion devours its prey. The walls were adorned with memories of past family members and decorated with only the rarest antiques. The clock on the wall read four thirty a.m. as the last sheet of paper disappeared into the abyss.

A puff on his cigar and long sip of his brandy celebrated the removal of one more obstacle. His quest to complete the biggest project ever to be attempted in the state of Florida was nearing its conclusion. *Just one more obstacle to go and it'll be done*, he thought, watching the cloud of cigar smoke circle its way toward the ceiling.

* * *

"Arnold," echoed a voice from the large foyer that led to the rest of the house. "Come on and get some sleep. You've been going through those papers all night."

The woman stepped farther into the room she had seldom entered until recently. The rich aroma of the Cuban Cohiba filled the air as her husband sat behind the large mahogany desk. Leather furniture filled the room. The strange family portraits gave the impression of watching her every movement. Many of the pictures dated as far back as the Civil War. They had never bothered her before, but ever since her unwelcome visits to the Judge's desk over the past few weeks they had all glared at her with a threatening eye.

"Go have another drink and go back to bed," was the order she received. "If I want your opinion, or help, I'll ask for it. But I see that as an unlikely occurrence." He took another long puff on his cigar, exhaling the smoke toward the once-beautiful woman standing in front of him, now aged by time and drink. She waved the noxious fumes away.

"I'm only asking, Arnold. I'm sorry you see my concern as a nuisance," she answered the man she had learned to loathe so many years ago.

He glared over his horn-rimmed glasses and gave no response.

"I don't understand you. I gave up everything for you all those years ago, and all you do now is ridicule me. I don't know how many times I can say I'm sorry we never were able to conceive. But we did try."

The Judge answered, "You didn't seem to have a problem with that white trash ex-husband of yours, did you?"

She thought about reminding him that the long-ago fertility tests had showed she wasn't the problem before he continued.

"By the way, I saw him the other day. He sends his best to you."

The woman stared at the Judge suspiciously before saying, "You saw Thomas? He's back in town after all these years?"

"Yes, he was. He couldn't stay long. I believe he was leaving on a very long trip, and he won't be returning." He glared at her with a devilish smile.

She continued, "I don't know. I've been a good wife to you. You just—"

"Stop your whining. You never wanted for anything. I never begrudged you anything you desired. You, on the other hand, couldn't deliver on your end of the bargain."

With that, Tucker's mother shook her head, turned, and slowly walked away, regretting the decision she had made to leave her family forty-two years ago for the thousandth time.

CHAPTER

46

Sun on the Beach is a charming little eatery sitting on the edge of the Atlantic Ocean. You can have your breakfast and sit and cradle your coffee while watching the waves roll in. On Sundays, you can even see local Florida artist Damien Share exhibit his talents along the beachfront. Craig and I stopped here for breakfast on our way back from the morgue.

"Sorry to drag you out of bed, away from Karla, so early this morning," Craig said, sipping his first cup of coffee. "But you're the only person I know who could positively ID this guy, whoever he was."

"Yeah, I know, Craig. It's just so strange. All this time you think you know someone, have a handle on everything, and then… voilà…everything goes topsy-turvy, and nothing is the way it seems. It's kinda scary."

"We took some prints before they took him away. We'll run them through the IAFIS database and see what turns up."

"The what?" I asked.

"The system the FBI uses to track all the bad guys, you numbskull," Craig explained with a grin. "I can't believe you've never heard of it."

"Anyway, I really thought I was a good judge of character. But this guy had me completely fooled, and that's what bothers me."

Our waitress delivered our meals: a western omelet for me with a side of bacon and three eggs sunny side up with extra toast for Craig.

"A little on the runny side, don't ya think?"

Craig smiled. "Ah, it's a real man's breakfast, not that mix of shit you have there. You really know how to ruin good eggs."

The waitress topped our coffees and drifted to the next table, smiling as she listened to the banter between Craig and me.

"How's Jessie making out after the other night?" Craig asked with genuine concern while slathering more butter on his toast.

"She's doing okay. As well as can be expected," I answered.

"I hope she stays away from that asshole kid. If you want, I'll put a tail on him and harass the little shit." Craig looked up from the attack on his eggs.

"Nah, Craig. I'm pretty sure she learned her lesson. Plus it knocked her mother down a few pegs. She'll keep a closer eye on whoever Jess associates with. She seemed to be more interested in the family of the guy Jessie was dating than the kid himself."

I waited a second before continuing, "I have to confess something."

He stopped and looked at me in anticipation, then grabbed a napkin and wiped his mouth. "Go on. What are you waiting for, the buildup of suspense?" he sneered.

"I was about to tell you in the car earlier before you stopped me from talking. It was also on the message you didn't get."

"Yeah, I stopped you from talking 'cause I don't trust anything anymore. After the mess we had with the Indian's skeleton beneath the dune a while back, it's hard not to be suspicious."

I agreed. "I went back to the area off 532 yesterday."

"You what? I told you to stay away from that area until I had a chance to look into it."

"I just couldn't resist. There's something so strangely familiar about the area. I can't get it out of my head. Almost like a feeling of déjà vu."

He looked at me as his eyes narrowed. "What else you got? Knowing you, there has to be more."

"There is." I took a sip of coffee and gazed at the azure sea for a second. "I went out there and had a hard time finding the entrance, really had to look. I found it by luck. The gate was chained shut and new foliage was placed at the entrance." He looked at me skeptically. "So I walked in and followed the road. Someone went to extraordinary lengths to cover it up. It was graded and hidden by a scattering of leaves and branches. Like the way we use to hide our fort along the river when we were kids." Craig stared at the curvy waitress as she walked by.

"Craig, I'm over here," I said, redirecting his attention back to me.

"Sorry, I was just wondering..."

"Anyway," I continued, "I followed the trail and made it to the spot we were at near the rundown shack. And you know what? It wasn't there."

He looked at me as if I had two heads. "What do you mean it wasn't there? It couldn't have just picked itself up and walked away."

191

"I don't have the foggiest idea. It was gone. The area was clean as a whistle. You could tell something was once there. Just a few tire tracks in the dirt, that's all. But the scariest part, there was an armed guy out there standing guard with a gun." I paused to take a breath. "I'm no expert, but it looked like military issue. A semi-automatic of some type. He told me, in no simple terms, that I was trespassing and needed to get the hell out."

He looked at me, dumbfounded. "No fucking way. You must have been in the wrong place."

"No, I wasn't," I countered. "And even if I was in the wrong place, who the hell was the guy in military fatigues standing guard?"

"I don't know who could be out there," he said. "I'll run a check on the area and see what reaction the deputy's report from the other night got from the brass when I report in."

"Well, while you're doing that I'm going to run my own check on the area. I bet you most people have no idea who all that property belongs to."

Craig raised his eyebrows as he mopped the dish with another piece of toast. "Good idea, Sherlock. Do some real investigative reporting and find out. You can check the county tax records at the library for a start. But don't go back out there alone."

"Something about this entire mess sounds screwy," I said, drinking my last sip of coffee. We both sat in silence, deep in our thoughts, before Craig quickly called us back to thinking about Doug.

"I was wondering, Tuck. You never had any inkling who that Doug character really was?" He dipped his last piece of toast in his remaining coffee and waited for me to swallow a mouthful of hash browns.

"I'm telling you, he was the nicest old fella you could ever meet. We had some good times and became pretty close. He even got into the habit of calling me son." I stopped for a moment, realizing what I said.

Then it hit me. The strange dream. The way he called me *son* and always being around. With all the confusion with Jessie, I had totally forgotten about the dream I had the other night until now. *Nah, couldn't be,* I thought, and went back to what I originally was saying. "He was just a cool old coot."

Craig answered, "Yeah, but I told you before, something just didn't feel right about the guy."

The waitress came to the table. "Would you like anything else?" I immediately knew she made a mistake asking that question.

"Well, darling," started Craig as we both smiled at each other.

"*Craig,*" I warned. He looked at me like a school boy and smiled his boyish grin.

"No, we're good."

She placed the check on the table. "Thank you. And come back and see us again."

Craig couldn't resist. "No, thank *you* for the exemplary service."

The pretty young lady smiled at his flirtatious comment.

"I'll take the bill," I said. "I've been promising to take my dad, here, out for some time now. He doesn't get a chance to get out of the old folks' home too often."

She giggled and walked over to a new couple that had seated themselves on the other side of the café.

"I think she likes me," Craig said, laughing as he watched her wiggle away.

"My ass she does. She's just looking for a nice tip, and you can leave that."

"Yeah, yeah. Whatever." Craig proceeded to remove a ten dollar bill from his wallet and place it on the table. He then took out his pen and began to write.

"What the hell you doing now?" I asked.

"Just leaving my phone number on the bill, with a little message to give me a call." He placed the pen back in his shirt pocket and smiled.

"Really, Craig? Really?" I just grinned, shook my head, and left.

CHAPTER

47

I had an hour to kill before heading over to the *Brevard Daily* office. Craig would be going back to headquarters to run a check on the area from the other night and see if the deputy's report had garnered any attention.

Karla had already left for work, so I kicked off my flip-flops, threw my keys on the kitchen counter, grabbed a towel from the stack of unpacked boxes, and headed to the shower.

"Damn." The spare bedroom looked like hell with all those boxes strewn all over the place. If I eventually didn't take a few minutes to unpack my few possessions, the room would remain a mess till Christmas.

Nah, maybe later, I thought as I stepped into the shower.

The warm water welcomed me as it bounced off my shoulders and trickled down my back. My mind rehashed all the events from the past forty-eight hours. I needed to piece together the reasons for Doug's death, or whoever he was. If I could do that, I'd at least be able to rest easier.

I shampooed and lathered. After a long, massaging rinse, I toweled off and threw on a pair of khaki shorts and a button-down Cubavera shirt.

Walking past the bedroom I figured I could wait for Karla to do this. *Ah, what the hell,* I thought, *might as well get some of this over with,* and dumped the contents of box number one on the mattress. Sheets and towels tumbled everywhere. It only took me a few minutes to fold everything and place them in the linen closet.

The second box contained assorted pieces of clothing that were not already hung on hangers in the closet. T-shirts, mismatched socks, and mesh shorts found their way into the first three dresser drawers.

Now that wasn't so hard, I thought.

I dumped the next one on the bed. Papers, books, and folders that substituted as my filing system for bills lay strewn across the mattress. I started to rearrange all the materials into separate piles when an envelope I had never seen before caught my eye. It was simply labeled "Son."

What the...?

My heart started to race and my palms started to sweat. I carefully removed the folded sheet of paper and read.

Tucker,

If you are reading this letter, then any hopes I had of speaking with you face to face have passed. I don't know where to begin. I have tried a number of times to tell you, but we got along so well, I was afraid of ruining the friendship we had developed.

Please read this entire letter before passing judgment on me.

Tucker, I'm really your father.

I stared at those words, *your father,* and felt myself becoming light-headed. I sat down, held my head in my hands, and composed myself before continuing.

I know this is as confusing for you as it is for me. But a very long time ago I found it necessary to remove myself from your and your grandmother's lives. It was the hardest decision I ever had to make.

After your mother divorced me, and with her marriage to Arnold Galley, things started to spiral out of control. Our family has very deep roots in Brevard County, and many individuals will go to extreme lengths to take it away from us.

Your uncle Peter was murdered in what everyone believed to be a boating accident. It was also intended for me, and I too was reported killed. As long as I was alive, you and your grandmother wouldn't have to worry about your safety. Your nan was kept in the dark until I visited her a few days before her passing. I hoped the less you both knew, the safer you'd both be.

There is so much I want to share with you. If I can't, there are two people you need to contact. The first is our family attorney in downtown Melbourne. His card is attached. The second is Helen Vanhise of Island Heights, New Jersey. Please see her, Tucker. She is an amazing woman. I would never have made it through the tough times without her.

There is also a lockbox in a hidden panel beneath my navigation station. It is unnoticeable to the naked eye. Measure eight inches in from the bulkhead and four inches below the settee. Slide and push to the right at the same time. It is spring loaded, and you need to use a great deal of pressure. All my memories, valuables, and keepsakes are in there, as well as my journal. They now belong to you.

Please be careful, Tucker. If I'm gone, you will be in grave danger. You are an excellent investigative reporter. Check into that area east of I-95. I am not completely sure why our land is so important, but you can find out.

I don't know if you have any type of relationship with your mother, but stay clear of her husband, Judge Galley. I believe he may have something to

do with my brother's death and the desire for our land. Remember, things
may not always be as they seem.

    Love you always.

    Dad

How long I sat, I couldn't tell you. Shadows had now crept across the bedroom floor, and sunlight reflected off the palms through my window.

I looked at the clock and realized ninety minutes had passed. The letter had been bittersweet. I still had a hard time believing all this and would need more proof than just a letter.

If true, I was glad my dad had survived the fiery accident…I mean murder. But I still had feelings of anger and sadness mixed with happiness. Why had he not stood up to those people and fought for what he believed rather than giving up his young son and leaving? Were the powers-to-be that strong? And what was with the land? Was he saying all that land belonged to us? Was that why I had feelings of déjà vu while out there? I needed to find out, and now I had a pretty good idea where to start.

CHAPTER

48

Attorney at Law Stephen A. Garvey's office was located on Grant Street just off New Haven in downtown Melbourne. I traveled the area numerous times while frequenting the bars and restaurants, but had never noticed anything resembling a law office.

I turned off Main Street and onto Grant, driving slowly and trying to match the building numbers to the one listed on the card my father left. I traveled about half a mile and found that the numbers started to fluctuate, showing no semblance of order. The mixture of old clapboard houses and newer, smaller buildings contributed to my confusion.

Damn numbers.

I swung the Jeep around and retraced my path. Finally I noticed it. A small shingle tied to a post introduced "The Garvey Law

Office" to any passer-by who would notice. I parked about thirty feet away in the first parallel spot.

A narrow cobblestone walkway led to a small yellow bungalow sitting off the street, sandwiched between two new larger glass structures. It reminded me of a moment caught in time; as progress enveloped the area, the Garvey Law Office survived and fought off the changes that the years brought.

I approached the front door, ready to knock when an elderly woman appeared at my side. She seemed to come out of nowhere.

"Can I help you?" she said. Wearing a gardening outfit, she rubbed her hands together to remove the dirt, then smiled.

"Yes, ma'am. I'm looking for a Mr. Garvey." I handed her the card I was recently given.

The elderly woman rubbed her hands on her calico apron before taking the card. She slid the glasses off her grey bonneted hair and onto the tip of her nose, reading the card with a stern expression on her face.

She handed the card back to me. "Sorry I'm such a mess. I've been tidying up the yard and adding a few shrubs to the garden."

I smiled. "You look lovely nonetheless, Ms...?"

"Ms. Garvey. Stephen's sister," she said, returning the smile.

"Oh, pleased to meet you. My name is Anderson, Tucker Lee Anderson." We shook hands.

At the mention of Anderson, Ms. Garvey's face froze. Only for an instant, but long enough for her face to become eerily familiar.

"I'm sorry, Mr. Anderson..."

"Please call me Tucker."

"Yes, Tucker, of course. Well, Tucker, my brother is away on vacation."

I showed the wave of disappointment on my face. She paused and then continued with a rejuvenated smile, "But he'll be back at the end of the week. My sister-in-law and he went on a cruise, out of the port, to celebrate their fiftieth wedding anniversary."

"Oh, that's wonderful. Do you think I can make an appointment to see him as soon as he gets back?"

Her grin turned into a broad smile. "Appointment? Well, let's see. How about you come back on Friday? We'll squeeze you in; let's say between nine a.m. and five p.m.?"

She totally confused me.

"Stephen has been retired for a number of years. He only services a few clients that he's had for most of his career. Just stop in. I'll tell him to expect you."

With that, I graciously accepted her hand again, thanked her for her time, and started down the path. I had a number of other places to visit before the day was over.

I spun around. "Excuse me, Ms. Garvey, I almost forgot..." I stopped in my tracks and froze. She was gone. How could a little old lady move away that quickly? I hadn't heard a door slam, and it was a good walk to the side of the house. So in the five seconds I had my back turned, where the hell could she have disappeared to?

CHAPTER

49

I fiddled with my keys as I walked back to the car, keeping an eye out for any movement by the elderly lady outside Garvey's office. There was none.

Ah, maybe I'm losing it.

I got in my Jeep and immediately saw the message light on my cell blinking.

"Hi, honey." It was from Karla. "Just got your message. So explain to me why you need a DNA test? The message you left was garbled. I had a hard time hearing the entire thing. Give me a call back. I'll have my cell on me. Love ya."

I started the Jeep and speed dialed Karla before pulling into traffic.

Yes, I know, I'm not supposed to do that.

She answered, "Okay, what the heck is going on? How much trouble did you and Craig get yourselves into this time? I just left you knuckleheads a few hours ago, so it can't be too bad." She giggled, then went silent.

I made a right turn on New Hampshire and continued through town.

"Karla, I need you to do me a favor."

"Okay, and it's—?"

"Is Doug's body still at the morgue?"

"Yes it is, but I'm not assigned to that autopsy, Bobby's handling it. Why?"

I had met Bobby at a holiday party a while back, and he seemed like an all right guy. According to Karla, he was exemplary in his job.

"Do you think you can trust him and get a look at the autopsy report?"

"Tucker," her voice trailed off before returning. "Those are two very strange questions. Of course I trust him, and I can see the autopsy report any time I want. I'm his boss, aren't I?"

I continued, ignoring her answer, "How long does a DNA test take to get back?" I made a left after the light and headed north on US 1.

"It depends," Karla answered. "The turnaround can take as few as a couple of days or as long as a couple of weeks. Now…will you please tell me what's going on?" Impatience was reflected in her voice.

"I'm sorry," I said, stopping myself from rambling. "I just need to confirm something."

"You're killing me here, Tucker. What is it?"

"After Craig dropped me off this morning, I had a little extra time to kill, so I started to straighten up the spare bedroom and empty out the boxes with all my stuff in them."

"Go ahead. Get to the point, and stop beating around the bush."

"I found a letter Doug placed in one of my boxes before he died. He must have put it there before I moved. You see, I need the test because…Doug said he's my father."

Karla didn't respond right away. An eerie silence hung in the air.

"Tucker, get up here as soon as you can. I'll be waiting."

CHAPTER

50

I made it to the medical examiner's office in less than twenty minutes, parked under a shady palm, and exited the Jeep. Walking toward the complex, I called Karla to let her know I had arrived. I didn't have to wait for her to answer. She emerged from a side door and approached me with quickening steps.

"Let's go and grab something to eat." She forced a smile and grabbed my arm, redirecting me back to my car.

From her actions, I knew something was wrong. I opened the passenger door to let her in before jumping around to the driver's side and strapping myself in.

"Now you tell me what's going on." I spoke first. "I can tell by your body language. Something's wrong."

She sat with her arms folded across her chest, looking straight ahead. "We'll talk when we sit down to eat," she said, not moving a muscle. We sat in silence for the short ride to a local sub shop.

"Just a cup of tea with lemon, please," she told the waitress as we settled into our booth in the back of the shop.

I looked at her in surprise after the waitress took my order for a short Italian sub and an unsweetened iced tea. "You told me you wanted something to eat. What happened?"

"No, I'm not hungry, just very concerned with developments at work."

I watched the corners of her mouth twitch with nervousness as the waitress returned with our drinks, then walked away snapping her gum.

"After I spoke to you, I went downstairs to see how Bobby was doing with the autopsy on Doug." She paused for just a second. "Turns out someone from the state prosecutor's office showed up and took the report."

"The report is gone?" I couldn't believe what I was hearing. "Is the body still there?"

"They're not quite that quick. I'm sure they'll come back later and collect the body. The good news is Bobby thought something wasn't on the up and up and made copies before handing over his results."

My sandwich arrived, but I too was no longer hungry.

"When Bobby told me everything that happened, I took a swab sample from the body to use for your DNA check. Just in case the body mysteriously happens to disappear. I have a vial and swab in my purse for the inside of your mouth. I'll take that sample before I go back."

I sat in silence, having nothing to add.

"I'll run the test through a friend I have in the Orange County office."

"Great," I said with relief. "So we're good then?"

"Well, I hope so. What bothers me, Tuck, is after all the crap you had to deal with last year, I've become very suspicious of anything that seems the slightest out of the normal routine." She pulled a sheet of paper out of her purse and slid it across the table. "According to the autopsy Bobby completed, Doug was dead before he hit the water."

"What? How could that be?"

She started to explain. "Well, whenever we have an apparent drowning victim, the first thing we check is how much water is in the lungs. Doug had very little, if any."

I sat mesmerized.

"When Bobby saw that, he immediately looked for other signs of death. Since he fell off his boat, he checked for contusions on the body, and it states right here," she pointed to a section of the report I couldn't see, "that no signs of trauma were found on the body. Of course he checked for signs of a heart attack too, but found nothing to indicate one."

We both sat in silence. I finally took a bite of my sandwich while she sipped her tea.

"So Bobby didn't find anything?"

"I wouldn't say that. I told you he's exceptional at what he does."

"So you going to keep it a secret? What'd he find?"

She shot me a sarcastic look and said, "Basically nothing at first. But after a closer examination, he found a small puncture, a needle hole, the kind a syringe makes, under the victim's armpit. That indicates he injected himself with something, or was injected. I sent out for a toxicology report. The only problem is it'll take a few weeks to get the test results back."

"I don't think he had any intention of killing himself. Especially after the letter he left for me." I'd totally forgotten about the letter in my back pocket, but now I pulled it out and handed it across the table. I managed to take another few bites of my sub as Karla sat and read the letter.

"Tucker, I'm scared." She handed the note back to me.

"You think?" I tried to crack a smile to relieve the tension, but she wanted no part of it.

"What are you going to do?" she asked.

"Well, I have a few things in mind. The lawyer won't be in till Friday. So I think I'll catch an early flight to New Jersey tomorrow. Hopefully I can get some answers up there."

She nodded her head in agreement.

"But before then, I want to check something out at the library. I'm more worried about you being alone at the condo while I'm gone. I'd rather you stay at your mom's place for a few nights until I get back. I should only be gone a day, maybe two."

She agreed again.

"You also have Craig's number. If anything in the slightest bit strange happens, go with your gut instinct, no matter how trivial it seems, and call him."

She said she would as I continued, "And it's important that you act as normal as possible when you get back to work."

I paid our tab and left the half-eaten sandwich on the table.

When we got back to her office, Karla gave me a long hug saying, "Please be careful and call me every couple of hours."

She disappeared into the complex, and I headed for the library to check a few things before leaving for New Jersey.

CHAPTER

51

I found a table at the rear of the Melbourne Library overlooking the river and set about reviewing every historical map of Florida I could lay my hands on. I had examined a number of maps months earlier, but at that time had only concentrated on the coastal part of Brevard County and Merritt Island. This time I needed to focus my attention on the entire state and the development of Central Florida.

I flipped through a number of old atlases and watched over time as small towns like Miami and Jacksonville transformed into mega-tropolises. Orlando, called a cow town by many old-timers, exploded out of dairy pastures to become one of the premier vacation destinations in the world. All this information I already knew and was not surprised to find.

Then I found it, or at least what I hoped would be it. I found a number of maps tucked away inside a large atlas, buried beneath a pile of old periodicals. The maps dated as far back as the 1800s, but one dated 1925 was the one I needed to see. At that time the state appeared to be carved into four sections: The Panhandle, bordered by Alabama and Georgia on the north and the Gulf of Mexico to the south, stretched all the way to the Oscilla River area near Tallahassee. The rest of the northern section reached to the Atlantic Ocean and as far south as a diagonal line cutting across the state from the Peace River, below Tampa, to the Daytona area. No unusual names or labels accompanied the sections, but to the south it was different.

The southernmost part of Florida, from the Peace River south, was labeled "Collier."

Hmm. I know there's a county named that, but it couldn't be as large today as it was a hundred years ago.

The central part of the state, from coast to coast, was labeled "Mosquitto," but had a small tag below it marked "Titusville Trust."

Time flew by and the clock on the wall signaled I had already been there for over two hours. I rubbed my eyes, headed over to the computer, and sat down to Google two names I hoped would be the missing pieces to the puzzle.

The first search was *Collier,* and as the screen flashed the results, a wealth of information fell at my fingertips.

Holy shit.

I found that Barron Collier had come to southern Florida in the early 1900s and bought over one million three hundred thousand acres, covering a major portion of South Florida. Today, two companies with strong business values engaged in agriculture, real estate, and oil and gas production operated there.

I paused for a second to make sure I really comprehended what I was reading.

Could it be? I thought to myself. *Damn, that's a lot of land.*

Even as a lifelong Floridian I never knew the area was involved with those businesses, especially oil. Now I really started to wonder. I printed out a few pages to read on my morning flight.

I spent the next half hour searching for *Titusville Trust* and finally found what I was looking for.

"No fucking way," I said out loud, getting annoyed looks from the people sitting nearby. What I had found was astonishing. The names listed in the trust were all too familiar. If everything I had read and was now thinking was true...then there were a number of reasons certain individuals would want my dad and me out of the picture.

CHAPTER

52

My flight continued to circle, waiting for its clearance to land at Newark International Airport. The deliberate, bumpy approach of the 737 was not something I was accustomed to. Flying is not my idea of relaxing transportation. Yeah, it's faster, but it's also a long way down from thirty thousand feet. The idea of dropping was not a pleasant thought.

I gazed out of the window as we dropped through the low cover of clouds. For as far as I could see there was a sprawl of houses, highways, businesses, oil tanks, and the skyscrapers of Manhattan in the distance. I had never been to New Jersey, and from what I'd been told of the state, it all seemed to live up to those expectations.

People actually live here? I thought as the wheels skidded on the runway.

After clearing the baggage claim area, I stepped outside to take a shuttle to my car rental. Wearing only my windbreaker, I was greeted by a cold drizzle.

Holy shit, this is really freaking cold.

I was amazed at the amount of traffic and maze of roads I needed to navigate just to leave the airport. The number of beeps and middle fingers I received as I maneuvered my way onto the New Jersey Turnpike was almost comical. Maybe rental cars should come with signs that say, "Relax, I'm new to the area, so get off my ass."

I found my way to the southbound lanes and accelerated to meet the flow of traffic.

The directions I had were to take exit 11 and connect with what they call the Garden State Parkway.

Garden, my ass, I've never seen so much cement and congestion in my life. They call this the Garden State? Shit.

With the theme of *The Sopranos* playing in my head, exit 11 came up sooner than expected. I paid my toll and connected with the southbound lanes of the parkway heading toward exit 82, Toms River, and a place called Island Heights.

At first the parkway was no different than the turnpike, lots of congestion and traffic. My wipers worked intermittently to keep the windshield free of the mist that froze between the wiper sweeps.

After crossing a massive bridge, I was suddenly surprised to see the roadway open up to a wide expanse of rolling hills. For early spring, the trees had started to bloom, and the once pale grass was starting to take on a green hue.

The ride actually became pleasant. I slowly distanced myself from the area they call Newark and started to see why New Jersey took the nickname the Garden State.

Maybe they should relocate their airport. The area really makes a bad first impression on visitors.

The highway rolled through the countryside and the sun began to peek through the clouds. A once dreary day now became bathed in sunshine.

I threw on my sunglasses and found a radio station to listen to as I traveled through Monmouth County and entered one called Ocean. The signal drifted away, so I played with the dial and finally settled on another station called WOBM. The music was light and the morning talk show hosts fun to listen to.

Exit 82 was now in my sights. I exited to Route 37 East. Once off, I pulled into the first gas station I came to.

Emerging from the vehicle, I picked up the pump and found a slot to place my credit card. Instead of the request for my pin, I got a message asking for a code number. I stood dumbfounded with the nozzle in my hand as a goofy-looking fellow approached.

"Hey, dude, what the hell? You trying to get me fired?" he shouted.

"No, I'm okay. Just trying to figure out the code number to turn the pump on."

He looked at me with a quizzical look on his face. "I got it, damn people are so impatient." He grabbed the nozzle from my hand.

"*No*, that's all right. I can handle it myself," I said, roughly snatching the nozzle and yanking it back.

"*No*, I'll get it," he said more forcefully and took the nozzle from my hand again.

What the hell? We playing tug-of-war here?

He continued to stare at me and seeing the confused look on my face finally said, "You're not from around here, are you?"

"No, what gave it away?"

With a smirk he continued, "For one thing, that tan you got there, and secondly you didn't realize there's no self-service in Jersey. I would have added the clothes, but there are a lot of dumbasses here that wear shorts all year long."

I stood there at a loss for words. I never considered myself tan. It was just the skin color I always had. And self-service? Was New Jersey the only state without it?

He realized I was at a loss and continued to speak in a friendlier tone. "What brings you here? Usually at this time of year everyone wants to high-tail it south for spring break. After four months of crappy weather, we all start getting a little cranky."

"I'm only here for a day, maybe two. Need to see a relative in Island Heights. How far away am I?"

"See a relative? You couldn't talk to them by phone? You needed to see what March is like at the Jersey Shore?" He laughed as he handed me my receipt.

"No. A relative just passed away. I need to see the family and deliver the bad news face to face."

"Oh, sorry to hear that, dude." He went on, "Island Heights... well, go about four more lights and hang a right into the U-turn, but don't go around the jug handle. Stay to the right and continue on Vaughn Avenue."

I thanked him and thought to myself, *What the hell is a jug handle?*

I continued east on Route 37, counting the lights. Finally arriving at Vaughn, I made my turn and drove a little farther until a sign welcomed me to Island Heights.

I was immediately taken aback by the quiet beauty of the small town and the rolling hills that ran along a river.

I followed my directions to the top of one hill, found the numbered house set amongst a few cut from the Victorian era, and parked my car on the street.

Sunshine was abundant, but not enough to ward off the chilly breeze that blew from the river along the hilltop.

I pulled on my windbreaker, exited the car, and walked to the surprisingly large house and rang the doorbell.

It felt like eternity, but finally the door opened slightly. An attractive woman, aged by time but still extremely pretty, answered the door.

"Hello, my name is—"

"Hi, Tucker, I've been waiting to meet you."

CHAPTER

53

Entering the hallway of the old Victorian, I noticed the smell of fresh baked goods wafting through the air. The home was warm compared to the March chill outside.

She stared at me for a second and finally said, "Tucker, my name is Helen." She reached to take my windbreaker. "Is this all you wore?" she said with a half-hearted laugh. "You are so your father."

"Yes, my father, Helen, that's what I came here to talk to you about," I said in a quiet tone.

Helen just smiled at me. She wore an apron around her waist, just as I always pictured a stay-at-home mother would look.

I continued to speak, "I'm afraid I have some unfortunate news for you."

She raised her hand to stop me from speaking and motioned me to sit down. I chose a chair near the corner window.

"Ironic that you would select that chair, it was your daddy's favorite. I was just about to have a cup of tea, would you like some?" She smiled as she went into the kitchen without waiting for my response.

I'm not a tea drinker, but in hopes of being gracious I intended to accept anything she put in front of me.

"Maybe a beer would be more suitable. Your dad would always have one when I offered tea." Her laugh echoed from the kitchen.

"No, Helen, tea will be fine. Just a touch of milk and sugar, thank you." I could hear her taking dishes from the cabinets. I let my eyes adjust to the dim lighting, accentuated by the early spring darkness outside. The living room was large and neatly decorated. A number of paintings and portraits hung on the walls. On a mantle that ran the entire length of a stone hearth sat family pictures. I got up and looked at a number of pictures of Helen and Doug, or should I say my father. They were all in various stages of aging. Most were taken at the beach or on a sailboat. Then I saw it, a picture like no other, followed by a number of others.

A young boy slowly grew into adulthood through these family memories. Nothing was unusual with his pictures until his teenage years. In many he was wearing football and basketball uniforms with the name CENTRAL printed across his chest. The thing that was unusual about the pictures was they were all of me. Let me rephrase that. The pictures weren't of me, but of a young man who looked exactly like me.

Helen returned with the tea and stood quietly behind me as I continued to gaze at the photographs. She saw the look of surprise on my face when I turned around. She said, "Tucker, that's your brother."

CHAPTER
54

I accepted the tea and sat back down in my dad's chair. Helen sat beside a coffee table across from me. We both sat in silence for a few seconds as Helen just stared at me. It was then I realized she must be looking at her son through my eyes.

"Helen," I needed to break the silence, "Doug, or should I say Dad, had an unfortunate accident."

She turned toward the door and said, "I knew that, Tucker, as soon as I saw you at the door. When you came up those steps alone, without your father, I knew…he had passed. I do need to know, Tucker, how it happened."

"He fell, Helen. He slipped on his sailboat, fell, and hit his head before falling into the water. There was nothing anyone could do. He was found the morning after."

"He fell?" came her surprised reply. "Tucker, he was too good a sailor to just slip and fall into the water. He could walk that deck and sail his boat through the roughest waters and darkest nights without a hitch. His falling shocks me."

"Well, the coroner is still finishing her autopsy, and I should know for sure in a day or two."

Again we sat in silence. Helen's eyes were glazed with a sheet of tears, but she kept her composure.

"Helen, I came here to inform you of Dad's passing, but I was hoping you could fill me in with some information about him. I was told at a young age, and honestly vaguely remember he had a boating accident and was killed."

Her eyes widened and she turned to face me. "Tucker, I was hoping you could fill me in as well. I'm at a loss about the secrets your father held. I only found out about you three years ago, after... after our son passed away."

I turned to look at the photos on the mantle and back at Helen.

"Your dad was a very quiet man, Tucker. When we met, I was coming off a very abusive marriage, and your dad made me feel like I was the most beautiful girl in the world. I knew I really wasn't." She smiled with a new light in her eyes as she recalled his kind words. "But your dad made me believe I was the most special person alive. He made me believe in love again."

She stared into space as she summarized the details of her earlier life.

"I also knew that your dad was running away from something. What, I'm not sure of, but I always felt there was something."

"I'm really not sure, Helen, what it was, but I do plan on finding it out."

She continued to talk as if I wasn't there. I guess it was like therapy for her, or her way of dealing with my bad news. "Your dad never mentioned you, but I knew someone important existed. He was in constant contact with someone in Florida…"

"My nan?" I broke in.

"No, I'm positive it was a male. I believe a man from Melbourne; a man I figure must have kept him abreast of your life. I say that because I overhead one of his conversations about a boy, and he said it was only an old friend who was telling him about his son. I even took the liberty to 'star sixty-nine' one of the calls and came up with the name Garvey. So it seemed plausible that it could have been an old friend."

I continued to listen to all this new information, remembering the name as the attorney listed on my dad's card.

"Anyway," she continued as I noticed her eyes glaze back into a trance, "your father had ghosts that haunted him. He slept restlessly and always seemed to be looking over his shoulder. He was only at ease when he was on the water. And then that all changed when Alex was born. We were older parents. I never thought I could bear a child, so Alex was a blessing. He filled the void that I now assume you left."

Her trance broke as she turned and looked into my eyes; I nodded, so she continued.

"Our lives revolved around Alex. He was a daddy's boy and did everything your father wished. He surfed, played every sport imaginable, and was an excellent student athlete at our local high school, Central Regional. He received every accolade one could receive. He had offers from many large universities. Then, at the start of his freshman year in college, he passed away. It devastated your dad and me. We never recovered from the loss. It was then I first heard about you."

She didn't go into a log of details, and I wasn't about to push her. I sat and let her talk.

"Your dad and I divorced two years later and he left. You don't go through a loss of a child and not have it affect you. I knew he found peace on the water, so one day he sailed away. He needed to re-find home, if there was one, and look for you. We haven't talked since."

"I'm sorry," I responded, not knowing what else to say. "Helen, I came here not knowing what I would find. I always was under the impression my dad died when I was five. My nan raised me, and I never had the slightest idea about any of this. My mother left us when I was very young, but I can tell by just talking with you for this short period of time, she wasn't half the women you are. It's obvious why my father loved you." I knew this was something she needed to hear and it was true.

She looked at me and smiled with appreciation in her eyes.

The time passed quickly and we talked a while longer, agreeing to stay in touch and keep each other informed of events.

Helen walked me to the door. We hugged for a moment before I stepped out into the icy rain of a New Jersey spring.

My mind was flooded with thoughts about my dad and the realization I had had a brother. It was heart wrenching to think these two people could have been a big part of my life if I had only known they existed.

Why then did my dad run off and leave me with my nan after my uncle was killed? If Doug was really my father, why didn't he tell me? All these questions were swirling in my head as I entered my rental car.

As I hit the ramp for the parkway, it was then I realized I was being followed by a large SUV.

CHAPTER

55

An unmarked patrol car sat around the bend on US 1, just north of Melbourne. The car sat slightly off the road beneath a cluster of palms—a usual tactic used by police to catch speeders. Although today the officer knew exactly who he was looking for.

It didn't take long for his prey to arrive. He had tailed the car for a number of days, and he knew the driver's daily routine.

The sports car finally zoomed around the corner and the radar gun registered eight miles over the limit.

Got ya, sucker.

The officer threw on his lights and pursued the vehicle for five hundred feet before pulling up behind the stopped BMW. He waited in his patrol car a few minutes to let the driver stew as he ran the tags through the computer.

Yep, that's my boy.

The officer walked slowly to the driver's window while performing the usual checks when approaching a suspect. "License and registration, please."

"I have it all right here, my man." The driver handed over the documents and added, "Yo, why you pulling me over anyway... Officer?" The driver snickered.

"You were clocked doing eight miles per hour over the speed limit."

"Wow, big deal. People speed on this road all the time, why don't you pull them over?"

"*Wayne* it says here. How long you been driving...Wayne? You should know the speed limit. Got any other paperwork?"

Wayne looked dumbfounded at first, then thought the pig must be asking for a bribe. He opened the center console and pulled out two twenties to hand to the officer.

"Put your hands on the wheel," yelled the officer as he placed one hand on his firearm and pointed the other at the wheel. "I said, put your hands on the wheel, now!"

Wayne froze, not knowing what to do next. As he sat there, he looked down into the open console and noticed what the officer had spotted: a bag of weed along with a few joints. "*Shit,*" he murmured to himself. "Damn, man, I swear those aren't mine."

"Yeah, that's what they all say. Get out of the car and keep your hands where I can see them."

"Really, man, you have no idea who you're messing with. My dad will have your badge for this."

"That's nice. I'll write that in my report as a threat."

The officer forcefully pushed Wayne onto the hood of the car and cuffed him. Before placing him in the rear of the patrol car he radioed for a tow truck to come get the vehicle.

"By the way, *my brother*, your car will now be towed and impounded."

Wayne's tone changed. "Please, dude, let's work something out. Can't you give a brother a break?"

Craig slammed the door and then pulled the mike out of the window to radio in his collar. *Piece of shit kid,* he thought with a smile. *I miss patrolling. Wait till I tell Tucker about this one. You never know who you'll meet on the road nowadays.*

CHAPTER 56

I changed planes in Atlanta and finally landed at Melbourne International. I immediately headed home for a quick shower and change of clothes before returning to Garvey's law office.

Before leaving the condo, I checked my mail and found a letter with the return address of one Stephen A. Garvey, Attorney at Law.

What's the chance of that? I thought to myself. The letter was short and to the point and asked for me to contact his office as soon as possible.

I hopped in my Jeep, headed to Grant Avenue, and found the small yellow clapboard house. I parked a few doors down and made my way up the cobblestone walkway to the front door. Climbing the two steps to the small covered porch, I opened the screen door and knocked three times. A middle-aged woman, different from the one I had previously spoken to, answered. "Welcome, Tucker."

What the hell? Am I the only one playing blindly in this game? Again I was shocked. How did someone I had never met before know me?

"Come on in, Mr. Garvey will see you shortly. Please have a seat."

This was no ordinary law office. The room looked like a flashback from the 1940s. Two large couches sat cattycorner facing a small desk. A grandfather clock ticked in the corner to break the silence, and numerous black-and-white photos adorned the walls.

After ten minutes a very old Stephen Garvey entered from a side door, munching on a sandwich.

"You are Tucker Lee Anderson. Yes, you are, you are," exclaimed the white-haired old man. He crept unsteadily to his desk, took a seat, and placed his sandwich on a napkin while wiping the crumbs off his shirt. I was mesmerized by his appearance. Pure white hair, bow tie, glasses hanging at the tip of his nose over a large, bushy mustache. His clothes were dated to match the room's ancient décor. He spoke aloud, seemingly oblivious to my presence.

"Let's see now," he went on. "Your Thomas's son and Gladys's grandson. Hum, hum. Lovely women she was, just lovely."

It was the first time I heard my father referred to as Thomas. It seemed as if I need not say anything to the old man. He was doing all the talking.

"Since the death of your grandmother and your pappy, the property in question is in the care of your mother and you. Yes it is. It's all written here." He flipped through a folder on his desk.

I spoke for the first time. "What property?"

It was then that he seemed to recognize my existence in the room. He looked over his wired spectacles to make eye contact with me. "Yours and your mama's land, the over one million acres your great-granddaddy purchased back in 1925."

CHAPTER
57

"You look surprised, son. No one ever told you about that property?" He had a very sincere look on his face as he repositioned himself in his chair and sat motionless.

"No, sir, this is the first I'm hearing of it, but are you talking about property that's located west of 95, along 520 and 532?" It was the property I had felt a connection with ever since my first visit to it weeks ago.

He energetically came back to life as he re-examined his folder, looked at me, and glanced back down again at some papers.

"On the twenty-first of June, 1925, your great-grandpa purchased that land for pennies on the dollar. He took a chance and speculated. The land never developed as he planned because of the marsh and ground composition. He was hoping to hit it big, as

Collier did in the south. But the area never developed, and the oil there was too hard to access, at least until now."

"Oil?" I responded in surprise. "There's oil out there?"

He appeared not to hear my question. "I was a young lawyer and new to the area when I met your grandpa. He hired me and my partner to take care of the legal documents for many of his ventures, and of course to handle the property. My partner and I had a difference of opinion and went our separate ways, but I stayed on as your grandpa's attorney. I had to do a lot to keep the land from my partner, who had planned to shadily take much of the property for his own."

A light went off in my head. "Excuse me, Mr. Garvey, your ex-partner wouldn't happen to be a certain judge that resides in the area, would he?"

He just stared at me. "I'm surprised, Tucker, I thought you knew all this."

The lawyer now laid the folder on his desk and turned to face me, elbows on the desk, hands clasped, and steel grey eyes boring into me.

"Tucker, when your great-grandpa died, everyone in Melbourne came out to honor him. He was so loved and respected by the community. The land was left to your grandma, and she willed it to your daddy and his brother, your uncle Peter. When your uncle was killed in the boating accident, everything was to go to your daddy after your grandmother passed."

Oh my God. It was all making sense now.

Mr. Garvey continued, "Tucker, there was one catch. Your daddy had a very bitter divorce when you were just a baby, and to get it over and done with, he gave half of the property to your mother as part of the divorce settlement so he could get custody of you. Only catch, she was to share the property with you upon his death. The one fly in the ointment, from my point of view, is that ex-partner of mine. He was your mother's lawyer and made it clear that he wanted your mother to have final say over everything in the event of her ex-husband's death. And you know their relationship now."

I sat in total shock. *Everything* was at first a haze, but now it all finally started to create a clear picture. The pieces of the puzzle were now falling into place.

"Sir, could you please tell me what happened to my dad? I can't put the pieces of that together. I do know it seems he stayed in contact with you all these years."

Garvey took off his spectacles and cleaned them with a tissue from his pocket. He began to speak while leaning back in his chair. "You can't quote me on anything I'm about to say, Tucker. It's all hearsay. You understand?"

"Yes, sir."

"Everything I'm about to say I'd deny in a court of law. Is that understood?"

Again I agreed.

"I truly believe your uncle was murdered. I can't prove it, but the boat explosion was no accident and was also intended for your daddy."

"But I always understood that my dad was killed in that explosion."

"You were a little boy, Tucker. Your uncle and daddy always sailed the river together at least once a week. The day in question, he wasn't on board. The explosion was intended for both of them."

I just listened as Garvey nervously played with his glasses, pulling them on and off his face.

"It seems certain individuals were all bent on taking control of your family's property." Garvey seemed lost in thought as he paused and gazed off into the distance.

"As I said," he continued, "you and your mama would get the land rights when your grandmother, uncle, and daddy were all dead. During and after the explosion, a number of threats were made against your family. Your daddy felt you and your nan would be better protected if he left and had certain individuals spend their time trying to locate him. As long as he was alive, he knew they would leave you alone. Your daddy recently surfaced after I contacted him. It came to my attention that papers were introduced into circuit court to have the land legally transferred solely into your mom's name, which would mean the Judge would gain control. My concern now is that you could be the next victim of an accident."

My skin started to crawl. I could feel my face redden as anger welled inside me.

We sat for a few moments more and discussed the legality of the documents in question. I told Garvey I wanted him to continue as my family lawyer and he agreed.

"Thank you, Mr. Garvey, for everything," I said, getting up to leave. "I appreciate all that you've done for me and my family."

He smiled and shook my hand with a vise-like grip. "Oh, by the way," I said, "please say hello to your sister for me. I hope her gardening project is going well."

He looked at me in confusion. "You want me to say hi to my sister?"

"Yes. Please do. The other day I stopped by, but you were away celebrating your fiftieth wedding anniversary. Congratulations, by the way."

He still appeared puzzled.

"Your sister was the only one here. She seems like a lovely woman."

He starred at me, and I continued. "A beautiful smile, short hair, round spectacles and a calico gardening dress. She told me to come back today to see you. I believe she was working out back on your shrubs."

He repeated his question. "You're saying you saw my sister and spoke to her? Tucker, my sister passed away some forty years ago."

I had to steady myself to keep from falling.

"She was very friendly with your grandma. My sister was a lovely woman. She took her own life as a result of a broken heart."

Garvey hung his head in sadness, and a tear rolled down his face as the memory of his sister began to surface. "She never recovered from the emotional pain she suffered. You see, Tucker, I too have an ax to grind with a certain judge. He wasn't only my partner, but also my sister's fiancé. He let greed dictate the direction of his life and in the process destroyed my sister."

"I...I don't know what to say."

"Don't say anything." My attorney smiled as life returned to his body. "You're not the first person to have seen her. She's a restless soul, and I find it comforting to hear she's still around."

I grinned and slowly reached for the door.

"Son," he spoke again. "I'm an old man. I no longer have any clients, but I promised Gladys I'd take care of you in the event circumstances changed. When this is all over, so am I. So please be careful."

CHAPTER
58

After doing my research and receiving the information I needed, I entered the premises from the south. It was the best way to gain access to the property along Tropical Trail that I had become so familiar with.

The small citrus grove provided ample cover as I maneuvered through the thick, knee-high grass. A full moon illuminated the sky, playing peek-a-boo from behind the low cover of clouds that introduced a cold front now moving in from the coast. A breeze blew off the river and rustled the palm branches just enough to hide my noisy, awkward steps.

Groves, my ass, I thought to myself. Though the fruit was seldom harvested, the large, expensive property kept a small orchard to use as a tax write-off. Seems if your property qualified and received a farm rating, your taxes were more than cut in half. You then received all kinds of grants to supplement your farming, whether you did it or not.

The owner of this property was sure to take advantage of every tax loophole he could find and skirt the local tax laws in any way possible. It was just another example of the rich getting richer and not paying their fair share.

Stepping from the last row of trees, I was sure to check for any kind of security system that ran along the edge of the immaculately landscaped lawn.

Craig had schooled me in every type of available alarm system. He also was able to tell me, from records he was privy to, that this property had a small laser system on the perimeter.

Craig wasn't crazy about my plan but went along with it anyway. He was in no position to accompany me, and getting a warrant for a high-profile figure such as this was impossible. Craig needed probable cause to enter the property, so he was waiting at the edge of the estate in case he was needed.

I found a low beam of blue light running along the boundary, low enough to go undetected but high enough not to be set off by small animals. The beams bounced from one relay station to the next.

I wriggled my body beneath the stream of light and entered the open lawn. No sirens. No spotlights. Everything was quiet, except for the sound the tropical breeze made as it raced through the foliage.

Walking slowly yet with purpose, I rounded the back of the house, past the pool to the area I was hoping would be my point of entry. Various landscape decorations were illuminated with lighting, which I was careful to avoid. I remained in the shadows and moved stealthily along. Another light reflected from the boathouse window to my right. I held my breath before exhaling in relief. A security guard stationed there watched his own personal TV instead of the security monitors.

The sliding glass door I sought was around the corner of the house, at an angle facing the pool. If I could trust the information I had been given, the door would be left unlocked. The information I needed would be in the large mahogany desk I sat across from only four months earlier.

A gentle pull of the handle, and the door slid open. Again I stopped and listened for the existence of any security devices. To my relief there were none.

Stepping into the room, I paused to allow my eyes time to adjust to the darkness. Shadows danced across the floor from the light of the moon reflecting through the windows.

There was the desk I was searching for. I stepped across the room and stopped behind it. With my pen light I illuminated the third drawer down on the right and pulled it open. There, with a number of other files, was one marked "Coastal Access."

I removed the file, slowly closed the drawer, and started to make my exit.

"Welcome, Tucker, I knew you'd eventually show up." An old, disgraced judge flicked the light on behind his recliner.

I was startled, and as my eyes took a moment to adjust to the bright light, I noticed a gun pointed at me.

CHAPTER 59

"I have to say, Tucker, you really have some set of balls to come walking in here like you're some hot shit reporter," came the words from Judge Galley. The longest-sitting corrupt politician in the state and the man I had exposed months earlier in my exposé. I was speechless, but only for a moment before I said, "Yes, I do! I have a large set. It's something I was born with or, should I say, inherited. I didn't need to steal them like you did."

The Judge laughed. "Yeah, okay, born with them? Your white trash father ran away and hid for forty years. I'd say that's one hell of a gene pool you've got there."

We both stared at each other, waiting to see what the other would do next.

"You know, Judge, you're not gonna get away with this plan of yours. You really think the people will stand for this kind of corruption and destruction of the land?"

"Oh, sorry, boy, I think they will," he sarcastically answered.

"You'll all be behind bars when—"

He cut me off with a curt, irritated voice. "You are so blind, Tucker. The people you speak of will label us heroes."

He smirked and continued, "You have no idea what you're dealing with. Do you think the oil in the Gulf of Mexico just comes from one isolated area? No, it's just the spigot to the entire well, and that well sits directly under the state of Florida. We are sitting on the largest reserve of oil in the world, but nobody has the balls to go after it. Our gutless politicians would rather let the Cubans lease their maritime areas for drilling to the Chinese, some that sit forty-five miles off our coast in the Florida Straits. And they're not the only foreign country involved. Oil is being drilled in our own backyard, and we're not doing it. If they can't drill directly down, they're drilling horizontally. Go look that up at the library."

"You're out of your mind. There's no way that could be kept a secret."

"No, Tucker. You are so naive. Collier found it years ago, and your great-grandfather had the foresight to see the future and purchase that land. Our geologists pinpoint that land as the center of the well. Too bad no one in your pathetic family had the sense of your great-granddad. Certain interests are holding back and waiting to reap the big cash reward when the rest of the world runs dry. I'm not waiting."

"Judge, it's not your decision to make. The people should decide. They'll have to live with all this in their own backyard."

Really, Tucker, the people? The people are idiots. They don't know what's good for them. When gas approaches six, seven, or even eight dollars or higher a gallon, do you really think they'll give a shit where we get oil from?" He paused for effect then continued. "The loss of some useless land will be a small price to pay for making us independent from foreign and radically controlled nations. So no, Tucker, you are wrong."

The eighty-two-year-old politician was now at the edge of his seat, gun still leveled at me.

I still challenged him, "When I break the story, I'll make sure to spell your name correctly, along with all your other cronies'."

He laughed even harder this time, and for the first time I noticed an eerie glaze come over his eyes as he stood and continued to keep his gun pointed at me.

"I don't think so, Tucker. That story will never go to print."

"Why, what you gonna do, shoot me?" I smirked.

"Exactly, Tucker. It's a shame you got shot during a home invasion. You know the law. You illegally gained access to my home. Out of pure fear for my safety, I had to shoot before being attacked. To my surprise, it was Tucker Lee Anderson. Your headline might read, 'Renegade Reporter Shot to Death by Terrified Homeowner.'"

I took a step back as the pistol was raised and steadied at me from fifteen feet away. For the first time in my life, I feared death. I held the folder tightly, closed my eyes, and winced at the sound of the shot.

* * *

I stood still, letting every sense come alive, feeling for the bullet within me, but oddly I felt no pain. Was I in shock? Is this how dying felt?

I opened my eyes, and across from me the Judge's eyes became large as he stared at me with a quizzical look on his face. He slowly lowered his arm and let his gun drop to the floor beside him.

Another shot rang through the night. This time blood gurgled from the corner of the Judge's lips as he fell to the floor, dead!

From behind the Judge emerged a woman. My mother, a beautiful woman, whom age and drink had unfortunately devastated, stood with her gun pointed where the Judge once stood.

Our eyes locked and she said, "I'm so sorry, Tucker, I'm so sorry for everything. Please forgive me and know I always loved you."

"NO, DON'T!" I screamed at the top of my lungs as the security guard and Craig ran into the room. My mother placed the gun into her mouth and pulled the trigger.

The Brevard Daily

"May We Check Your Oil?"

First in a Three-Part Series

Tucker Lee Anderson – Investigative Reporter

Imagine you're driving down Interstate 95 on a beautiful Florida morning, sunglasses on, wind blowing through your hair and the company of your loved ones riding along with you. Nothing could be better.

You pass the interchange for Route 528 and continue into Brevard County, that pristine region better known in history as the home of America's space race.

Then it hits you. You smell it before you can see it. The odor of crude oil assaults your senses as you finally notice a change in the landscape west of the highway.

A skeleton rises from the earth. You can't believe your eyes as one oil rig appears, followed by another, then another, until there are so many, you can't keep count.

Hard to believe there could be such a sight?

Well, if certain individuals had their way, the future of Central Florida and Brevard County would be changed forever.

This reporter has uncovered a plot that would have one of the country's biggest oil exploration projects take place right here in our own backyard.

A conglomerate headed by recently deceased Judge Arnold Galley had an amendment waiting for Bill S-550, first enacted in 1997, that would have given the rights to drill for oil to their organization, and then to many of the world's largest oil companies.

The group of investors, headed by the judge, used coercion and murder to aid in their quest to acquire over 1.5 million acres of Central Florida real estate.

At this time, the land in question is in the trust of one Gladys Anderson's family.

The article and subsequent stories went into depth detailing the Judge's and his associates' plans. The murder-suicide of Judge Arnold Galley and his wife was told as a loveless marriage gone bad. The powers-that-be wanted the story told that way, and I agreed. No reason to beat a dead horse.

As for the members of the Coastal Access group the Judge headed, no one faced any charges for their part in the plan. Many used their political clout, scattered and played the proverbial game of "cover your ass."

The head of World Wide Security Corp., Colonel Trout, was tracked down and arrested with his lead operative, Jack Prescott. Both have been charged with three counts of murder and are now awaiting trial.

As for a third operative named Jesus Rodriguez, it's believed he left the country and his whereabouts are unknown.

But we know better, don't we?

* * *

"Well, Nana," I said while I sat and looked out over the water, "I hope you can hear me. I just want to give you an update on everything."

I shaded my eyes as a large sailboat drifted down the river. "Carl and Jessie are doing fine. Carl is surfing and doing pretty well in

NSSA competition. He wants a statue of himself erected next to his idol, Kelly Slater, in Cocoa Beach." I laughed.

"Nan, you'd be proud of Jessie. She's become quite the young lady and now dates an academic all-American from Satellite High. He's not from a prominent family, but he's a hell of a nice kid.

"As for me? Karla and I are doing just fine. There's no ring on her finger yet, but she might be the one."

I whipped a tear from my eye and took a deep breath before continuing. "One thing I remember you telling me, Nan, is to not look at things and say what if, but rather look at them and be thankful for what they are. Love you, Nan."

With that, I slowly collected my thoughts, got up off the bench, and walked away from the river and out of the park Nana took me to as a child.

EPILOGUE

The spring rain ran down the windows of my office as I sat staring out into the cool gray morning. I had come into the office way before normal hours. I couldn't sleep anyway, so why not get a jump-start on the day.

I spent the first hour looking back over all the anonymous messages I had received about the property over the last few weeks. Only the last message, which had given me the location of the file I wanted, gave any indication that my informant was...my mother.

My mother had finally had enough of the Judge and his plans, but unbeknownst to her, the Judge tracked every e-mail and cell phone call she made. So my showing up at his back door was not at all a surprise to him and exactly what he wanted. Everything went as planned for him until my mother took it upon herself to put an end to his sordid past.

My story, "Coastal Access," had hit the news a day later, and my detailed stories were eagerly awaited by the public. It also went global with the help of Linda Greenwood, who made it the headline of the *U.S. Globe's* international edition. For her efforts, she was promoted to chief assistant editor for the *Globe.* And for the *Brevard Daily,* the lucrative financial windfall kept Mitch smiling from ear to ear.

Once again just about every news agency around—and not just from Florida, but the country and the world—decided to center their broadcasts on our quiet little Florida community.

"Morning, Tuck," came the greeting as Mitch stepped into my office and closed the door. I nodded hello.

"Listen, Tucker, I know how painful this must have been for you, or still is, but—"

I cut him off. "No, Mitch, you have no idea."

He gazed and continued, "Tuck, you know I love ya, and I think the world of you. If this is too much for you, well, we'll let the story go and hand it over to another news agency."

Mitch caught me totally by surprise with his comment, because operating in the black was all that mattered to him. This story was making the paper a lot of money, along with all the new advertising it would bring in for months to come.

I smiled. "Really, Mitch? You'd give it all up and take a loss on the revenue we could generate from the magnitude of publishing this story?"

Now it was Mitch's turn to smile. "Well, I didn't say I wouldn't charge a hefty price from another news agency."

We both let out a good belly laugh that I needed. "No, Mitch, that's not necessary, I'm a big boy. It's my story and it's…what it is. At least I'll get the chance to set the truth straight."

"I appreciate it, Tuck. If there's anything you need, just let me know," he said as he opened the door to leave and Jessie walked in.

"Hi, Uncle Mitch," she said with a smile, giving him a big hug.

"You got one hell of a daddy there, young lady, you should be proud."

"Oh, I am. I definitely am," she said as Mitch smiled and closed the door behind her.

"Hi, baby," I said with a smile as she came over and kissed me on the forehead. "What brings you here to the office so early?"

"Oh, Karla dropped me in front, she's parking the car."

Karla and Jessie together. *Oh no, this is a little strange. Do I have more disturbing bad news coming my way?*

"You two came together? Why?"

Jessie smiled. "Yeah, Dad, we drove over to Desoto and you weren't there, so we figured you came here to the office early; looks like we guessed right."

Karla entered, looked at Jessie, and then back at me with a nice big grin.

Jessie continued, "We figured we'd take you out for a little brunch and celebrate."

"Celebrate? Well, I guess we could. I'm really not in the mood for celebrating this story, but having my favorite two girls with me will compensate nicely."

"You didn't tell him?" Karla said as she smiled at Jessie.

"No, I was waiting for you."

Okay, something's going on here, and the only reason I am not freaking out is the smile on their faces.

"You two look like the cats that caught the mouse. What are you guys up to?"

They both smiled.

"Well, Dad, we won't be celebrating the news story, we have something even better."

"Go ahead, tell him, Jess," came the quiet response from Karla, who almost appeared giddy.

"No, you do it," Jessie answered.

I broke in, "Okay, you two. You both are driving me crazy, fess up. What do you two know that I don't?"

Karla nodded to Jessie.

"Okay," Jessie continued, "I'm going to be an older sister."

"Yeah, you are an older sister, you and—"

All of a sudden it hit me. I looked over at Karla and she just beamed with delight.

"You're…You're…"

"Yes, Tucker, you're going to be a daddy again!"

With that revelation, we had a group hug, and I'll be honest, we even cried a little. As we headed out the door, the words of my nan rang in my ears. *Family is all connected. No matter how big, small, or separated over time.*

ACKNOWLEDGMENTS

Many thanks go out to everyone who encouraged me in the creation of *Coastal Access*. To my family and especially Michele, you have continued to be my backbone and foundation along the way. A special thanks to Patricia Sperber for being my test reader.

A special thank you to everyone at the Writer's Workshop, especially John, Len, Bob, Mark and Richard, as well as all the others for their continuous support and positive feedback.

Walter Ramsay
If you loved Tucker Lee Anderson, check him out in
Walter's first novel, ***Beneath The Dune***
For more information visit:
www.walterramsay.com
www.penabeachpress.com

www.ingramcontent.com/pod-product-compliance
Lightning Source LLC
Chambersburg PA
CBHW060800120626
46557CB00001B/43